December Midnights
A HOLIDAY NOVELLA

VICTORIA WILDER

Edited by NiceGirlNaughtyEdits

Cover Designed by Echo Grace, Wildheart Graphics

Copyright © 2023 by Victoria Wilder

All rights reserved.

No part of this book may be reproduced in any form or by any electronic or mechanical means, including information storage and retrieval systems, without written permission from the author, except for the use of brief quotations in a book review.

For anyone who looks at the holiday season and hopes for a little bit of magic...

And for the rest of us who want the magic AND the grumpy, sexy man who only smiles for you, calls you baby girl, and knows what it means to warm you up.

Happy holidays, gorgeous.

PRELUDE

Along the coastline and waterways of Maine, there are more than sixty lighthouses. In the northern oceanside town of Wild Tide, one lighthouse in particular has many purposes.

To most, it's simply a light for ships and fishermen to see the shore, and know that the closer they come, the shallower and more dangerous it might be.

The children in this part of the north are told a fanciful story. That this lighthouse shines the very first light Santa sees as he embarks on his Christmas Eve journey. And then the last, guiding him due north for home just as dawn breaks on Christmas Day.

And to a few more open-minded believers, this lighthouse serves as a beacon of sorts. A talisman for the matchmaker who lives on its grounds. Its pull is meant to call and beckon lovers. An unexplained force connecting soulmates and giving them a fighting chance at their happily ever after.

Time and fate never seem to be on the same side, so this was the compromise. A lighthouse at the tip of the world, with the northeastern winds at its back and the North Star at its front.

It's a place where time moves differently, and the practicalities of elements can work in a way that feels a little spectacular and a lot like *magic*.

CHAPTER 1

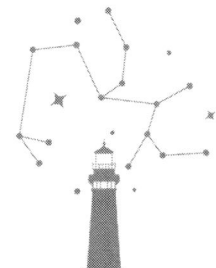

GRAY

The way I hate endings is for this exact reason. The questions. The "what's next?" and "how does it feel?" All the optimistic bullshit glossing over the idea that something great is now done. I fucking despise the need to tell someone a lie that whatever is next will be better. It won't be, I guarantee it.

"You're not telling me there's been no one."

I run my thumb along the worn leather of the club chair, trying not to let the reality of the answer get to me. Nobody else would get away with asking me this question except my brother. I jerk my head to the right just enough to answer.

"Anyone? Anyone?" He leans forward, elbows on his knees, ready to hear that I'm lying. I knew having drinks would turn into this. Typically, we stay busy enough that the details of our personal lives aren't the focal point. He's a talker and over-sharer. I'm not.

It's been almost two years now since I've been with someone. What he doesn't know is that it's worse than that. I haven't *wanted* a single person I've crossed paths with. Not one.

"Since her? You haven't even rebounded, like, with…anyone?"

I keep quiet as I stare at him. More questions won't garner a different answer.

He shouldn't be all that surprised. I spend most of my time with him. It's not a far stretch if he really thinks about it. Most of my friends cleared out after my breakup. And the rest disappeared after my injury. Aside from West, most people hate me now.

"You think it's smart to start messing with people who are staying here?" I don't even look at where he's looking. I know my brother. There's a blonde that's likely been eye-fucking him since we sat down. "We've been here for"—I look at my watch—"less than eight hours. You don't want to settle in before you fuck a local?"

"'Is it *smart*?' isn't the question I typically ask myself when I see someone I like." Smiling at me with his usual charm, it's hard not to smile back. "But…wouldn't it be smart to fuck a local to settle in better?" He wiggles his eyebrows.

"You're an asshole."

"Never said I wasn't." He drains the rest of his beer and stands. "We're practically townies now anyway." We had a few weeks in the late summer, and again in October, sorting out our investments. And while we're paying taxes and upgrading businesses in Wild Tide, I wouldn't consider us townies. We're barely tourists.

"You can laugh with me, Gray. No one is watching."

And that's just it. Any time I relax or feel a sense of calm, someone does. Watches. And I never know if it's going to be a fan. Someone looking for an autograph or a dickhead who starts chanting: *"You're a taker, a breaker, a love faker, but you could never deliver. You could never make her...get there."*

Fucking lyrics.

"I haven't heard it since we've been here. So stop thinking about it."

I flick my narrowed eyes up to him. "I'm not."

"You are. When you do, you get these deep lines right next to your eyebrows."

Not many people want to go out with someone whose new reputation labels them as "a disappointment" or "a piece of shit." So, I avoid strangers and crowds if I can. Hell, I've moved us to bum-fuck Maine to get away from anything that resembled the life I used to have and love.

West holds his arms out to the sides, palms up. "Let it go, Gray. Nobody cares here—I mean, look around. It's the jolliest fucking place I've ever seen. People are more likely to ask you about cookie recipes than if you used to date the one we shall not name."

I hold back a laugh. I'm pretty set on being a cranky asshole for the foreseeable future. Keeps most people from thinking twice about approaching me that way.

I look around at our investment anyway. It is pretty fucking festive here. The Timekeeper Inn feels like Christmas dipped in bourbon. Cozy and welcoming, the smell of cinnamon and pine winds its way throughout the main room and beyond from the moment you step inside. The walls are dripping in varying types of greenery, all wrapped in deep red ribbons. Vintage sconces and candles illuminate every wall and surface, even clustered across the built-in bookshelves and bar. My shoulders relax a pinch while the bourbon warms me from the inside out, as I take in the atmosphere. All of it makes it harder to keep my guard up.

He scratches at his jawline, eyes darting around the room. I'm not interested in what he's up to. And I get it. I used to be. Flirting with women was second nature. Tack on being a professional baseball player for one of the most talked about teams, and it made flirting, never mind fucking, *too* easy.

We're going to be here for the next few weeks through the holidays, working on renovations, plans for expansion, and it made sense to just stay on premise. But I'm not planning on staying here all that long afterwards, and the last thing I want is to hook up with a stranger.

West sits forward and mumbles, "Incoming." But I don't catch it before I'm flanked by two women on either side of my club chair.

"Gentlemen, whatever it is you're talking about over here could really use a shot to go with it," a redhead says as she looks between us. "Thought you might like to buy us one and tell us what's so interesting."

Great.

West smiles, leaning right into their advance. "We were just talking about how beautiful the women in this town are."

They both laugh. I hate the way it sounds—sickly sweet and void of any real emotion. It's the same old thing. Flirt. Fake. Fuck. And then sometimes it turns into a pile of shit relationships built on superficial compatibility. *No thanks.*

"They are beautiful, aren't they?" the owner of The Timekeeper Inn says as she sashays into our conversation.

Attractive, not beautiful.

"Wild Tide girls tend to be something special, in my opinion."

I'm relieved at the interruption, regardless of how inaccurate the opinion might be.

"Ms. Archer," West says, standing and giving her a hug and kiss, like he's known her for ages. I'd only just met her when we arrived a couple of hours ago. And before that, any of my dealings with her were through our attorney and financial advisors. West came to look at the place once. They're not friends, but they are putting on a show as if they were.

"West, darling." She gives me a side-eye glance before continuing. "Gray," she nods. "I have a delicious batch of blackberry brandy I'm sampling before I turn in for the night. Would you fine folks like to try one up at the bar with me?"

Nope.

The two women and West are already standing. Winking my way, she leads them from this spot in front of the fireplace.

Natasha Archer is an interesting woman. If I had to guess, she's in her early fifties. She reminds me of a brunette Stevie Nicks, her long hair braided in random sections. She dresses like she's just been to a renaissance fair, with scarves and various materials hanging from her dress. A lot of jewelry. She doesn't look like a businesswoman, but she gave us a run for our money during negotiations. The woman knows exactly what she has here: aside from the inn, a functioning lighthouse that's been a pillar of this coastline, hundreds of acres of untouched property along the bluffs, and some commercial property along the docks that line the harbor on the other side of the property.

The things we had to agree to in order to execute the investment had me wondering why the hell we were doing it, but ultimately, there's a lot that can be done here. And there's sentimental value. That was the kicker, and she knew it.

I drain what's left of my glass and slump back into the chair. Pinching the bridge of my nose, I try to tamp down the dull headache that seems to have taken up permanent residence behind my eyes. It's been a year of headaches and constant anxiety, working out the anger that's come with the shitshow that has become my life. When my therapist suggested I find a place outside of Boston, it made sense. I didn't need to stay in a city that doesn't feel like mine anymore. My constant knee pain is enough of a never-ending reminder of how different my life is now. It's the one thing I can't run away from—no pun intended. I barely remember what it was like not to limp, or to feel a throbbing so fierce that it wakes me up from a dead sleep.

When I look over at the clock, it's almost midnight. I'm finally feeling like I could pass out as soon as my head hits the pillow. Getting up, I make my way to the staircase, not looking back at the bar. West is there drinking and having a good time, and I don't want to think of an excuse for why I don't want to join. I'd rather sleep off my mood and start tomorrow with a fresh outlook on this place. But, as soon as my foot hits the first step up to my room, there's a clanging of pots and pans that stops me. Down the hallway toward the oak-stained double doors, where the kitchen is located.

"Mr. Turner."

I turn back toward the voice. "Ms. Archer."

She bats at the air. "Oh please, call me Tash."

Tilting my chin down, I nod.

"If you'd like a little midnight snack, there's always something in the kitchen for you." She gestures to the doors that just had my attention.

"I'll pass. I'm going to head to bed."

The way she says it has me curious, though. Like she doesn't only mean milk and cookies.

When I take another step, she hurriedly asks, "Can I ask for some help tomorrow by chance? I could use some extra brawn if you wouldn't mind."

She knows we're here for planning and renovations.

West and I want to roll our sleeves up and do some of the labor. It's too big of an undertaking for just the two of us, but it's part of the reason we're here. Long before baseball, we both worked for my father's construction business. It feels good to fall back into that type of hard work.

I give her another nod.

"Excellent. See you in the morning, Mr. Turner."

"Gray." But she's gone before I can correct her.

I could go for something to eat now that she mentioned it. As I head toward the kitchen, only about three steps from the door, I hear a woman's laugh. It's light, surrounded by the sound of a horse neighing and The Ronettes—why I know who sings that song is beyond me. But for some reason, my lips twitch with a smile even before seeing what might be so funny.

When I push the doors open, it's not the smell of cinnamon and coffee that has my mouth watering. Or the Christmas music playing and being sung along to that has my ears heating. This full body reaction is in response to the swaying of rounded hips and full lips spouting off the chorus of lovely weather and ting-a-ling'ing.

The room is easily twenty degrees warmer, but I can't seem to do anything–not even roll up my sleeves, never mind interrupt. I can only watch this sprite of a woman glide around the floor, while carelessly dropping used spoons and bowls into the overflowing sink. She moves on to whipping something white and creamy in another bowl. I don't question why I want to dip my finger in it and watch to see if she'll lick it off. I just stand there.

Dumbstruck. A bit enamored. Entirely turned on. She's like a magnet, and I'm being pulled right to her, instantly forgetting what the hell I was doing before this.

A minute or two ticks by before she looks up. She does a double take, spotting me leaning against the doorway, watching her back.

She looks like trouble. The kind I know is going to mess with me.

She doesn't stop what she's doing. Instead, she keeps her eyes locked on mine for only a moment, and fuck do I feel it everywhere. Looking back down at what she's mixing, she says, "You're bigger than I thought you'd be." I'm not sure what that means, but I don't even care to decipher it. I'm too caught up in her presence. She lets go of the spoon and wipes her hands on the frilly red apron tied around her waist. "I'm not complaining, don't get me wrong."

A wide, bright smile reaches her eyes and hits me right in the chest. I try my hardest to hold back from mirroring it in response, but the corner of my mouth ticks up, and that's enough of a cue for her to keep talking.

"Want to try something for me? Tell me if it's too sweet."

Despite the fact that I haven't said a word, I'm eager to try whatever she's offering. I take in the wild blonde hair piled high in a knot, curls trying their hardest to escape whatever is holding them in place. Doing exactly as she asks, I dig my hands into my pockets and find myself standing across from her in just a few strides.

A tiny speck of a diamond pierces her nose, and a deep dimple cuts in on her lower right cheek. And if those were her only standout features, she'd be cute, adorable even. But pair those with her big hazel eyes, more golds and greens than the browns and blues of mine, along with pouty lips that look almost ripe enough to bite, and she's sexy too. Altogether, she's the most beautiful thing I've ever seen. I'm a bit pissed off about it in all honesty. She wasn't what I planned to find on my way to bed tonight.

She dips her finger in the white, drippy frosting, then holds it up like she heard my unspoken request from a moment ago, and wants me to lick it off her finger. And yeah, this isn't normal behavior between strangers, I know that, but I couldn't care less.

"I need to know if it's too sugary. I've added cardamom and cinnamon, but I've already sampled so much I can't tell if it's good or I'm just riding a sugar high."

I look down at her finger, and then at her mouth. When her tongue peeks out for a moment, that simple move has me sucking in a breath. Warming my chest. Stiffening my cock.

With a tilt of her chin, she moves her finger just a bit closer. "Try it for me?" she says softly, and it's already a done deal.

I lean closer, part my lips, and let her slide her finger into my mouth. The sugar and spices coat my tongue instantly. With my eyes locked on hers, I see exactly what it does to her. Her face flushes pink, spreading down to her neck as she swallows. I feel the same heat, only it's all over me. Down the back of my neck and rushing to my front, my cock fucking jumping against my jeans. *Yeah, I feel it.*

A small sound escapes her lips as they part, watching my mouth slide down her skin. She slowly pulls her finger back, but dammit, I'm not ready for that yet.

I grab her wrist, hold it in place, then drag my tongue along the length of her finger. Our eyes connect, her arm relaxing in my grip as she seems to lean closer. I couldn't tell you if there's a world happening out of this room because nothing outside of this moment exists for me. For just a few seconds, everything in my life feels inconsequential compared to this insanely hot and unexpected moment with a stranger.

When I let her go, she takes that finger and runs it across her lips without pause. A primal feeling takes over me at the sight, so much so that a growl slips past, one that I didn't even know I was capable of making.

AURORA

I felt an instant attraction the moment he entered the room, as if every nerve ending in my body had been shaken awake. I didn't need to look up to know it was *him*—exactly the person I'd been expecting.

It's mid-December, and this is my month. I was told it would happen, so I had expected a little flutter of acknowledgment. Maybe a zing like I've read about in books, but nothing like *that*. I have my eccentric moments, but sticking fingers in strangers' mouths is not a typical occurrence for me.

The glide of his tongue, the wrapping of his lips along my skin...I felt it everywhere, along every inch of me.

I wanted to taste what he tasted, so I let my tongue slip across the line of my bottom lip. I've done all the talking. In fact, he hasn't said a word to me, but right now, I keep my eyes on him, trying my best to stay in this moment for as long as possible. I feel myself moving toward him, like my body's acting of its own volition to be closer.

Looking away, he finds the bowl of frosting I was just whisking and runs his thumb along the edge. *Please, let's play this game.* It's my turn now. Without thinking, I open my mouth as an invitation. A chance to reciprocate. His eyebrows turn down, like he's warring about what he wants. But then the most subtle smirk graces his face as he brings his thumb to his own mouth and gives it a quick suck. *Tease.*

"I can taste orange zest mixed with cinnamon," he says. His voice is deep and low, a timbre that I feel like a caress. I like how it sounds as it settles around us.

I smile big because he got it right. Few people can pick out the little taste notes in the breakfast treats I like to make for guests, but he almost got all of it. "There's something else. Any guesses?"

I shouldn't be surprised that he doesn't say anything. He brings his finger to the edge of the bowl again.

The corner of his mouth tilts up, partially hidden by

his overgrown beard. There's something satisfyingly sexy about how it frames the outline of his lips. If I hadn't caught it at the right moment, I would have missed it.

I lick along my bottom lip again, tasting just a hint of what I smeared there a minute ago. My body warmed from the tips of my fingers to the center of my chest. The way he leans so confidently against the counter, watching me so closely, has me feeling bold and brazen. Like I could demand this man take what he wants from me and it'd be the most fulfilling experience of my life.

"I want a taste," I say quietly as I sway closer.

"Do you?" The low, roughened tone hits me right at my core this time as his smirk converts into a half smile. He very much approves of my request.

Instead of dipping his thumb into my waiting mouth, he slowly closes the gap between us, runs his frosting dipped thumb along his own tongue, and then grips my chin. He searches my eyes for permission as he pulls me closer.

His mouth hovers a breath away, but my body started screeching "yes" the moment he walked in here. So I close the distance and press my lips to his, a quiver tingling in my belly at the sensation. My arms wrap around his shoulders as his wind around my waist. When his tongue collides with mine, the taste of sugary cinnamon floods my senses, and we both share a moan.

In the same fluid motion, he lifts me onto the counter like I'm light as a feather, not breaking our connection. I wrap my legs around his body, and he molds himself to me. *Damn, he's strong.* One hand snakes up and into my hair with the lightest tug, as the other grips my hip, then my waist, smoothing across my back. The kiss is urgent and out of our control, like this is a feeling we've both been waiting for. The groan that escapes him between breaths settles along every inch of me.

Pulling me closer, the hand on my nape tilts me to where he wants. With a hum, I welcome every touch point. My breasts firmly press to his chest. My legs tighten around his hips. My nails dig into his shoulders. He's so much bigger than me. His masculine scent of bourbon and pine only adds to my daze. *Goddesses, I can't get enough.*

The bark of a laugh and a high-pitched yelp has us pulling back from each other, smiling for a brief moment at what we had just let escalate.

"This," a man's voice pipes in from the threshold of the kitchen. He points and wiggles his finger right and left between the two of us, "is not what I was expecting to find." He looks at my stranger and smiles. "See, Gray, smart is overrated."

"Fuck off, West," he grounds out.

A loud, drunken cackle comes from under the arm that he has draped on the doorway. And I know that laugh. It's *not* one of my favorites. "Oh my gosh, Aurora. It smells so good in here." When she sees my stranger, she audibly gasps, and grips the knot of her wrap dress. Bethany Goodwin is easily the most animated and flirtatious person in Wild Tide. She also is the quickest to gossip and badmouth behind someone's back. It's not a lifestyle I subscribe to, especially considering some things I've witnessed growing up with Tash. "You're the guy!"

I hear him whisper to himself, *"Fuck."*

I glance between the two men again. How would she know that he's *my* guy?

But before she can say anything more, the man who interrupted us wraps his arm around her middle and lifts her off the ground, backing out the way they came in. "Let's go. I need you and your friend to show me exactly how to do those sun salutations you keep talking about."

I hear her laugh again as he leads her down the hall.

"My brother," he says with a slight roll of his eyes.

I smile. "I couldn't tell." I rub my palm against my cheek. "Your beard. But now that you've said it, I can see it."

Nodding, he gives me a reserved, close-lipped smile. I sway closer to him, feeling drunk from that kiss. *I want more.*

"Are you here early? For the Winter Solstice?" I ask. He has to be here for me. It's the only explanation.

"I don't know about Winter Solstice," he says, his finger still tracing my pinky. The only part of us still connected after the interruption.

He presses his free hand to his chest. "I'm Gray. I'm here because I own the place."

I bark a laugh, a knee-jerk reaction, then speak without thinking. "The fuck you do," I blurt out.

His eyebrows shoot high, surprised, maybe even taken back by it. Most people mistake my optimistic demeanor and think I don't swear like the sailors who pass through. It's a very inaccurate assumption.

"Aurora," Tash interrupts, gliding through the doors. "Oh, Mr. Turner. I see you came looking for that snack after all." Flitting by me, she looks at me the way she does when she knows she's reading a situation correctly. She plucks the teakettle from the stove, which has just started to whistle.

"Gray," he corrects, and I feel like it's not the first time.

Tash gives him a once-over as she makes a heavy pour of bourbon in her mug. She leans over the counter and snags a dried orange slice. "I'm glad you two finally met."

"But he's not here for the Winter Solstice."

Watching me for a minute, she reads between the lines. *He's not here for me, is he?*

And her answer pierces me. Sharp and quick. "Mr. Turner is here to help us out."

"Us?" he asks, looking at me again, confusion and intrigue clear in his gaze.

His attention feels like nothing I've ever had the privilege of feeling before.

Wait, what did she just say?

Tash answers him, nodding at me. "Aurora lives here. She's my family. Helps me run–"

I cut her off, "What do you mean *'help us out?'*"

It's written all over her face. We aren't meeting the necessary payments to keep our loans. I try to supplement as best I can with the things I make and sell, but it's not steady. And after the last hurricane that swooped in and caused damage, we needed to borrow more. Solstice and Christmas always bring a flood of people, but Wild Tide is a seaside town. Most people don't want to be on the ocean or beachside during the wintertime in Maine.

"The Turner brothers are our new investors." She waves her hand in a circle like she isn't dropping a bomb on me. "Which makes them part owners. Partners."

"Tash…" I cover my mouth when I say it, shaking my head in denial. I thought he was here for me. "You think it's a good idea to bring in strangers and just–"

"This is my place, Aurora. They'll be here to help us get out from under a mountain of debt that I won't ever be able to pay off. And to help us make some necessary adjustments to improve what I've put off for too long."

Gray looks between us, quiet and observing.

Moving on, she pours the boiled water into her mug. Tash is good at glossing things over. "Aurora, I think we should grab more Christmas lights before we get the tree tomorrow, don't you think?"

I untie my apron with a huff, hopping down off the counter. *How could she have made this huge decision without me?* "That's it?" Throwing my hands up, they flap down at my sides. "We're just talking about holiday illumination now?"

"You're being dramatic."

"You just sold a piece of who you are." I try to tamp down the emotion that's surfacing, but my voice cracks beyond my control. "Who *we* are."

I try not to look back at Gray. I don't want him to see

how upset I am. He can't hear what I really want to say to her. I want to rewind. I want to lean into him and pick up at the exact moment where we left off before being interrupted. A few minutes ago, he was a stranger. A possibility. But now...

I need to get out of this kitchen. I'm halfway through the mudroom before I hear his deep voice following close behind me. "Don't leave," he says. There is a vulnerability in his tone that has me stopping mid-step.

When I spin around, I collide with his chest. I keep my eyes focused on the dark buttons of his buffalo plaid shirt. I like how much bigger he is than me. It's not intimidating, it's comforting. "I thought you were someone else. I shouldn't have... I apologize."

"Who?" he asks curtly.

"Doesn't matter." Tilting my head back, I meet his glare. I let out a short laugh at how ridiculous he must think I am. "I don't typically do things like that with random men."

His mouth tilts up, like he's amused. With his impossibly deep voice, he says, "Tell me."

I take a deep breath, shaky with emotions that I'm unsure how to process. And that must register instantly because his eyebrows pinch together and the quirk of his lip straightens, replaced with something that looks more like concern. I turn away again, unable to answer him, because honestly, this feels like too much to process at the moment. And maybe I'm being dramatic, but really, what the heck have I just done?

I decide not to linger any longer, so I grab my jacket

and head out the door. I'll be better if I breathe the ocean air. I need to cool the chaotic thoughts ripping through my mind. *He's not here for me.* How did I go from one moment of ease and contentment to this same-as-always feeling of uncertainty.

The feeling of relief and excitement of who this man could have been to me is long gone. That kiss. I touch my lips, still feeling the tingle from his mouth and beard. He's not here for me, even though it feels like he's exactly who I've been waiting for. I shake my head, tilt my chin up to look up at my stars. How am I supposed to forget how that just felt? This is my December, which means there's someone coming that I'm meant to kiss instead.

"Goddesses," I whisper out. The plumes of my breath, visible in the cold, are more of a plea than just a passing word. Somehow, I need to convince myself that I can still be kissed by someone who *isn't* Gray Turner.

CHAPTER 2

AURORA

The front door slams open much more aggressively than I was planning. And with it comes a rush of flurries carried in from the ocean winds. Maybe it's my extra enthusiasm and eagerness to talk to Tash. But it's enough to make the ladder leaning against the stairs rattle, and a few of the books piled along the edges of the stairs topple over. The small crystals from the vintage chandelier hanging in the foyer sway from side to side. It announces my arrival with a chime as the small glass pieces clink against each other.

"Tash?" I look to the front sitting room of The Timekeeper Inn. Empty. I skipped breakfast this morning and rushed out to figure out what was left to do for Solstice and Christmas. I needed the distraction. Something to keep my hands busy. I'm still salty about last night. The idea that she would keep something so important about this business from me has me annoyed, but it also hurts. This is my home too.

I move down the hall, past the stairs. Nobody. I peek into our main room, consisting of our bar and lounge, where most guests spend time outside their rooms. The massive stone fireplace is lit. But that room is empty, too.

The low trumpets and piano riff of Louis Armstrong singing about taking a trip from Coney Island while the moon is bright makes me smile. She's here somewhere.

"Tash?" I peer around the pantry. Empty.

She's not in the kitchen, but I hear muffled voices from the greenhouse connected to the back of the house. I don't think about it before I do it, even though I should know better than to interrupt.

I'm pummeled with a blast of warm air when the door swings open. The smell of cedar and lavender hit me instantly. But it's the birch root that has my eyes widening. *Shit*. Between the excitement thrumming through me and the gallop I did down the stairs, my momentum wouldn't let me turn around before being seen.

"Aurora–" It's not just Tash in the greenhouse.

"For goodness' sake. Natasha, you told me we wouldn't be–"

"Hello. I'm so sorry." I smile softly and keep my attention trained on Tash. The funny thing about the people in this town is they have no problem giving Tash shit for being a matchmaker, but they also want her time when she's willing to give it. And I get it. She has the ability to connect people. And sometimes help others with practical matters. An elixir for keeping colds away, a salve to keep a lover coming back, or a bunch of carefully selected herbs to burn that'll banish negative vibes from your home. I just hate when people are two-faced. Good enough to pay her for her gifts, but never good enough to invite her to Sunday brunch or even exchange pleasantries at the farmers' market.

Wild Tide is my home, but some like to pretend not to know us. For instance, I'm going to pretend not to see the owner of Whip & Drizzle asking Tash to help her daughter find the right one. The birch root gave it away. And in turn, Tash and I will never pay for another pastry or drink when we stop into the downtown coffee shop. Unspoken agreements that I've gotten used to accepting over the years.

"I'll be sure to knock next time. Apologies."

Tash leans back in her chair and pulls deeply from her vape pen. "We're done here anyway." Holding out her palm, she waits for her payment. "I'll get a better sense of her timing once the Winter Solstice is over." She shifts her eyes back to me, just briefly. She does it because it's *my* year. And I shouldn't know that, but I suppose it's one of the perks of being raised by a soulmate-level matchmaker. I get the inside scoop on my own happily ever after.

I don't stay for the rest. Instead, I keep myself busy in the kitchen, soaking the cranberries in orange juice and then adding sugar and mint to a packed jar of blackberries.

"You're in a better mood today," Tash says from the doorway.

I smile down at my hands and take a deep breath. "Is it him?"

"Who?"

I raise my eyebrows and smile wide. "*Him*."

She takes another pull from her vape as she watches me. Tash is not my birth mother, but by all accounts of her raising and caring for me, she's my family. And I know this look. It's the *you think you know something, but you don't know shit* look.

The smell of cotton candy peppers the air around the room as she exhales. "You already know what I'm going to say, Aurora."

I roll my eyes and turn toward the refrigerator, pulling out a bowl of grapes that have been soaking in lemon juice. These will be perfect for candying later.

"I'm telling you, Tash. This was different–I *felt* it."

"Like the two fishermen from two summers ago?"

I squint at her with a sarcastic smile. "No. And that was not...*this*. They weren't him. I mean, you saw him, right?" Opening my mouth, I give her a mocked surprised face. "Big and gruff." I raise my hand above my head, because he towered over me. "That beard and his forearms, jeez!" I laugh out loud, but it's more like a schoolgirl giggle as I picture him again, how attracted I was to him with just one look. "And he's got an edge, like if the wrong person crosses him..."

At my widening eyes, she holds up her hand. "I'm just going to remind you that there are more possibilities coming. I think you would be smart to keep your options, and mind, open."

"But I–" I try to interrupt, but she talks over me.

"Did you know that you can have more than one soulmate? It's not common, but it's not rare either. And I worry, my darling girl, you have this pull that makes it so easy for people to want to be near you. To want to fall in love with you. And if you're not paying attention to the difference between attraction and—"

"I know the difference."

"Magic," she finishes, as if I didn't interrupt her. And she says it so casually, like it's not the one word we try to avoid saying out loud. Not because we don't believe in it, but because the word is attributed to fantasy and folklore. Tash always says that people like to minimize unexplainable things they don't understand. We don't operate like that here. So we believe in it, but we never say it.

"You said the 'M' word."

"It was warranted. And I need you to pay attention, Aurora. This isn't something to be cavalier about."

I'm really trying to rein in my emotions, but I'm failing wildly. Between last night with Gray and the fact that this place I've called home is not just ours anymore, it's a lot to take in at once. "I understand what you're saying. But I'm not a kid, Tash."

Her eyebrows shoot north. We never argue or bicker, but I know what I felt, and I don't appreciate her questioning my judgment.

Before I can say any more, she spouts, "You're right.

You're not." She grabs two mugs from the cupboard, pulls out a bottle of her homemade gin, and pours some in each.

"It's not even noon," I say, looking at her heavy pours.

She waves at the air in front of her, passing one to me. "Time is subjective, you know that."

I can't help but laugh a little. She really is one of the most enjoyable people in the world. She's impossible to stay mad at.

"I'm sorry I didn't tell you about the investors."

"It's your place, Tash." I toss back the gin in my cup—so much burning.

"It's not just mine anymore. It's been ours ever since you arrived, darlin'. But things sometimes need to change in order to move forward." She laughs at herself, and then studies my face. She always knows what I'm feeling, sometimes before I even do. "You're nervous."

"Be honest with me. Is this going to be our last Christmas here?" I take another breath and look around. "Are we going to be homeless?" My pulse ticks higher as I spiral. "I love that lighthouse. It's my space. They can't just come in here and make it look like..." Before I realize it, I'm breathing so fast that my vision gets blurry.

Pinch.

"Ouch! Fuck."

"Knock it off," Tash says roughly.

"That hurt!" I rub my arm where she plucked at my skin.

"What's gotten into you?" She leans against the

counter, brow lifting as she searches my face. "Goddesses, Aurora, I've never seen you get this worked up about something. Maybe there is something," she pauses, eyes narrowed in thought, "different here."

"You poured me a drink and made it seem like you were either going to tell me it's not my year after all or something worse."

She smiles at me, and I don't know how she does it, but it calms me instantly. "This is not a bad thing. And we're not being evicted. I would never allow anyone to take this place from us. But I'm smart enough to know when I need help. So I took it. I know what I'm doing."

I exhale and wipe the moisture from under my eyes.

"They've promised not to interfere with how we run this place, but they want to renovate, re-launch, and try to make it more tourist-friendly for the summer rush."

That sounds annoyingly optimistic. And also, like gentrification.

Rubbing my arms, she pulls me into a hug. "This is how it has to be. Sometimes, we need help. And when we find someone who's willing to give it, you welcome that opportunity and make the best of it." She gives me a shit-eating grin. "And don't worry, I gave them a run for it. Those boys had to agree to quite a roster of things in order to take part ownership."

And while that should make me feel better, it doesn't. Maybe my nerves about being homeless are waning, but not the fact that I went ahead and had the best kiss of my life... with possibly the wrong person.

"And this is very much your year."

I hear her and smile, letting it seep in. Is it better to know when your partner is coming or is it better to be blindsided by it?

"When you say renovations, does that mean they're going to paint everything white and decorate with seashells and–" I pinch the bridge of my nose, cringing. "And shiplap?"

"You think I'm going to allow any of that to happen? You know better than to think I'd let a couple of men come here and tell me how to run my house."

She's right. I can't picture it.

The same way I can't picture just pretending Gray Turner isn't going to be more to me than just part owner of my home.

We make our way out to the truck and Tash snags the keys from me. Help me, goddesses, because the woman drives like brakes and stop signs are merely suggestions.

"Don't forget your goodies for Bo. Let's see if we can work a little bit of–"

I give her a side-eye. There's no way she's going to say it again.

"Don't look at me like that, Aurora. I was going to say *hustle*. Work a little hustle."

I smile, because she was absolutely going to say magic. And really, I can't stop thinking that magic is exactly what I'm feeling.

CHAPTER 3

GRAY

The brightest thing I had seen in a long time was wearing a red fringed jacket and a tight pair of ripped and faded blue jeans. And her wild blonde hair was barely contained by her big furry hat. Not much makes me smile these days, but she seems to be an exception. Hearing her sweet voice this morning, negotiating a barter of muffins and soaps for a blue spruce, one cracks my face effortlessly.

She was clearly upset after learning exactly who I was, and I understood it, but it didn't keep me from looking for her this morning. I still feel her legs wrapped around me and my cock hasn't forgotten how she felt rubbing up against it either. I've barely looked at a woman in years and now I'm looking for and smiling over this one in a matter of hours, never mind kissing her in mere moments of meeting her.

"Holy high in the heavens." I hear a gasp behind me. None other than Midge Parrish, the owner of Wild Tide's souvenir shop. I'm not sure I've said more than three words to her, but I know all the places she's traveled with her husband, the names of her grandkids, and exactly where she feels her arthritis the most. In addition to The Timekeeper Inn, West and I now own most of Wild Tide's downtown commercial real estate. The second we swung the first sledgehammer in the strip of businesses next to her shop, she was at the door with a tin of butter cookies and dozens of questions.

I shift my eyes to her interruption.

I'd rather not draw attention to myself if I can help it. I'm here to escape being at the center of anything resembling gossip.

She clutches her purse straps and asks, "Are you? Was that…?"

Giving her a side-eye, I bite my tongue, refraining from telling Midge to shut the hell up—there's nothing to see. Aurora hasn't noticed me yet, and I still haven't figured out what I'm going to say to her when she does. So yes, I would rather drive a nail through my eye socket than let on to who has caught my interest enough to *almost* smile.

"It was. I swear I saw it. You're such a nice-looking man, even with that beard. And I know everyone has a problem with you boys coming in and gobbling up all that real estate, but I think it's good for this place. Fresh eyes. New ideas." She flaps her hand in the air and adds, "You should smile more. That brother of yours is always smiling. My goodness, he's a handsome one. Is he around here somewhere?"

She twists her head around to see if anyone else may have heard her, like she was running a public service announcement as the self-appointed town crier. But the only two people within earshot are heavy into a bartering discussion. Peering back toward the lines of trees, seeking out West, she turns back to me too quickly.

Crap, I need to get away from this woman, but just as I go to move out of the line, I hear the tree farm owner say, "Darlin', I can't barter. I've got a bottom line on these trees I have to meet."

"Oh," Aurora says, looking down at her cart and back up at him.

I'll be honest, I've never wanted to deck an old man more in my whole life than for turning her offer down.

She nods like it's no big deal and smiles anyway. "Maybe you'll change your mind. I'll still leave these soaps with you. They have that eucalyptus and mint that you like. It'll clear you right out when a seasonal cold shows up unexpectedly."

And just as she says it, he starts sneezing. Three in succession.

Nice timing.

The golds and greens of big hazel eyes peer over at me. And it's the same as it was less than twelve hours ago. I can't keep my eyes off her. "You followin' me, Mr. Turner?"

Fuck, her saying my name like that just did something to me.

I clear my throat, shifting my stance a bit. But I don't answer her. Instead, I talk to the dick who's not taking what she's offering. "I've got it. Whatever she wants."

Her eyes rake down to where I've pulled out my wallet.

"The tree is seventy-five dollars," he says, fingering through the hundreds I've just handed him.

"That's for the tree and whatever else she decides to take home."

Midge chimes in as if she's a part of this discussion. "See, I knew you were a nice man, even if you don't say much. That beard really is intimidating, too, but…"

Aurora leans into my personal space, cutting me off from hearing anything else the woman behind me rambles on about. My body sways slightly toward her, like if I'm closer, everything will be better. When her shoulder brushes into my chest, I have to hold back from wrapping my arm around her and pulling her against me.

"Don't you just love it when people tell you how pretty you'd be if you just smiled more?" She winks. Turning her head back, body still leaning into mine, she says, "Bo, I'm going to let Tash know that we ended up settling this through Mr. Turner here. But go ahead and keep those soaps."

He mumbles, "Sure thing. Thanks, Aurora."

I wonder if these two women have more of a pull in this town that they let on. It sure feels that way from this exchange.

She gives me one more look, the kind that says,

"You're going to want to watch me walk away." And I fucking do. I didn't notice until she was about ten strides ahead, but there are rips in her jeans, just below her ass, that show off the most delectable crease of skin. My mouth waters, hands remembering what it was like to hold on to her. They flex involuntarily at my sides, wanting to feel her again. Yeah, I'd take my time running my tongue along those paths of skin.

"She's a sweetheart," Midge mumbles behind me. *Cold fucking bucket of water.*

Then Aurora looks at me from over her shoulder. Her eyes trailing from my boots to my hat before she says, "Grab a saw, Mr. Turner. You bought it, you cut it."

The cold hits my nose and makes my eyes water, knocking me out of the stupor that staring at her had put me under. It's cold in Boston. Especially when the wind whips along the water. But this far north in Maine, surrounded by the ocean on so many sides, is a new level of chill, redefining the word *cold* for me. I move as quickly as I can over the packed-down snow. I never used to be so slow. My knee will never be the same again, and it has me swallowing a groan of frustration.

I hustle from a brisk walk into a jog, and then wince at how tight my knee feels. *Fuck, it's going to be sore just from that later.*

"Aurora," I call out.

She stops next to a bright red pickup truck and turns to me with a smile. I didn't take the time last night to think about her age. She's definitely younger than me, probably in her early twenties, if I had to guess. Another reason why staying away is the smarter idea, if I've got a good ten years on her. She pulls thick gloves from the truck bed. "I'm sorry for acting like that last night. I had expected...well, honestly, I wasn't expecting you. And then, hearing the news that Tash just casually dropped, it threw me for a loop."

We start walking toward the endless rows of evergreen trees along the matted down pathway that's a mix of mud and snow.

"I wasn't expecting you either." *Or the way it felt to kiss you.*

She tilts her head down, nodding toward my knee. "Did you hurt yourself?"

I look down at it, like it isn't the source of all my bullshit. I never talk about how much it hurts, and I didn't think I was being obvious about how I favor it. I fucking hate it. "Yeah, I injured it playing ball." I tell her honestly, surprising myself when I add, "Had a couple surgeries, so now I can at least walk on it, but it's sore most of the time."

"You're the baseball player." Her eyebrows raise as realization hits. She didn't know who I was. At all. Beyond just a new investor in The Timekeeper. "Everyone talks about you."

The words make my gut lurch. I don't want to know what people say about me here, especially when she's around to hear it. For some reason, her hearing negative things, regardless of how misconstrued they might be, bothers me more than usual.

"One of the best baseball players Boston has," she

says, tilting her head to the side, almost sounding proud to repeat it. I don't correct her that it should be past tense. That's all over now. "Everyone said your parents met here. Fell in love right here in Wild Tide... One of the Solstice matches." She shrugs, brushing a curl away from her cheek. "Not many, if any, famous people come from here, so you're as close as it gets to being a hometown celebrity."

"Not a celebrity," I correct. "Just a baseball player." It comes out rougher than I want, but I'm not interested in being anything more than a baseball player. I ignore the fact that I'm not even that anymore.

She nods and stays quiet after that, and it has me stewing about what else she said. I don't know the exact details of where my parents met, only that they loved Wild Tide because it brought them together. They would have called it home if they had more flexibility with their jobs. My dad moved a lot for work, and my mom, before she had my brother and me, was in the Air Force. They didn't have much of a choice about where they lived, but they talked about where they wanted to be eventually. Wild Tide was always a part of their plan–they just never got the chance.

I let that sink in. How good it feels not to hear negative shit about me for once.

"Solstice matches?"

She nods again, searching my face for a reason why I'd be asking. But then her pretty eyes track down to my lips.

It's almost like the cold wind takes a break from blowing for a minute as we stop walking toward the rows of trees. When I swallow, she follows that movement, too. That dimple that peeked out last night pinches on her cheek again when she rubs her lips together.

Fuck, do I want to pick up where we left off.

"I have a really good soak with salts and herbs that might ease that knee pain. A balm, too, that might be nice to have after a long day. I'll put something together for you."

I don't know why, but her offering thaws a part of me. "You'll make it?"

She hums, biting her lip.

I don't know why that hits me square in the chest. Maybe it's that she's doing something for me, to make me feel better with no other motive than to ease what causes me so much aggravation. "I'll try it."

Her responding smile is the kind of payment I'd take any day.

"Do you sell those types of things at The Timekeeper?" I ask, interest piqued.

"It's more of a little hobby. I sell some of it online, but it's more of a thing that keeps me busy than anything serious." The way she says it, I have a feeling she's downplaying her talents.

"You should think about having your stuff available for guests. Locally made products, exclusive to the inn, could be something original The Timekeeper offers."

She doesn't say anything right away. Instead, she leans forward and wraps her arms around my shoulders. When she holds me a pulse tighter, it warms me instantly. A heat that runs from the back of my neck up to my ears. I clear my throat as my hands find her waist. Her chest takes in a deep inhale and a drawn-out exhale, the delicate fingers at the nape of my neck gliding into my hair.

Jesus, that feels nice.

I close my eyes, and my body relaxes one muscle at a time with her wrapped around me. I can't remember the last time I've hugged someone for more than a brief moment. The way this woman makes me feel is something far more familiar than a stranger.

As she leans back, her arms still draped around me, she searches my eyes. Her head tilts slightly, eyebrows pinched like she's questioning what just happened or maybe looking for something. Her fingers brush away the hair that's fallen forward from my forehead. I feel like a pet being praised and revered as the tips of her fingers graze my skin.

When a sudden gust of wind whips her hair into her face, she laughs out, "You feel that?"

I'm feeling many things I haven't felt in a long while, or maybe ever. Some I'd buried before my life started to unravel and some I'd locked up after my injury. But I feel something here, something palpable, and I know if I'm not careful, it'll do more damage. The only issue with that is I can't decide if the idea of being a nobody to somebody is the kind of damage that does something good. A forced change to the shit I've been wading through.

"Maybe." I bite down, jaw clenching. *Fuck*, I'm flirting. But damn, it feels good to do it.

She smiles, dimple and all. Stepping back, she pushes her hair out of her face. I miss her hands on me as soon as they're gone. "The northern winds that come off the Atlantic are always the ones that seem to be the most intrusive, don't you think?"

Reaching up, I gently push a few strands that keep blowing back into her eyes up into her hat. Her light gaze meets mine, and the emotion dancing around her features makes it impossible not to mimic. How could I know a person for only hours and feel such ease with them?

She looks down at my lips, the same way I'm practically studying hers. She whispers, just loud enough for me to hear, "I'd like another taste, too."

My phone buzzes in my pocket, breaking the moment, giving me an out that I really don't want. *What am I doing?*

"I need to take this."

When I pull away from her, I instantly regret it as she wraps her arms around herself and gives me a placating smile.

My agent sighs as he says, "Gray," on a sigh. I already know whatever I'm going to hear isn't going to be what I want.

I add a little more distance away from Aurora.

"Hunt, tell me it's starting to die off," I say in the most even tone I can muster.

"Gray, give me a fuckin' break here. I've been working my damn PR team overtime, trying to tamp down your bullshit. But you decided you wanted to date a damn country singer and then break up with her," he says in his thick Boston accent. We've known each other for a long time, and I trust he's working on it, but I want my career to end on my terms. It took so long for me to get to that level, and I can't accept that a rookie and a bad call during The World Series cost me the game, my knee, and my career.

"Hunt–"

"Don't fucking *Hunt* me, Gray. If you want to sue for slander or libel, that's up to your attorney, but my job is to salvage your brand and the name you built in the MLB. Not this shit about being a disappointing boyfriend. I knew it wasn't a good idea to date her in the first place."

I expel a heavy breath. "That's incredibly unhelpful. And you know we both ended it, right? That she was the one who wanted to have an open relationship, and I said I didn't want to hold on to something that wasn't there."

"You don't need to convince me that she's in the wrong here, but it doesn't change the fact that you have millions of people who hear your name now and don't think about the number of World Series games you helped lead Boston to. They only care about the current discussion, which is the country song that's crossed over to pop charts and has been sitting at number one for weeks. And the source of her broken heart and unsatisfied soul is Y.O.U."

He groans, and I can just about picture him rubbing a hand down his tired face. "If you want a coaching position that isn't on some farm team in bum-fuck nowhere, then you need to lay low and let me do my job."

"How long?"

"Until I call you. When I do—"

I cut him off, "*If* you do, you mean."

"Listen, diva, if you need a pep talk, then look to your brother for that shit. You'll know I've got you something good when I call you. In the meantime, don't get in anybody's face—"

"That prick shouted in my face first—" I counter.

Some asshat thought I wouldn't hear him calling me names and telling his buddies I should have been traded. Unlucky for him, I did, and I don't believe in letting people run their mouths when they're just plain wrong. So, I told him to tell me that to my face, with a few curses thrown in for good measure. Someone recorded it, and then it was another wave of bad publicity.

Hunt keeps talking, and when I look back to where I walked away from Aurora, she's gone. I hope she didn't overhear any of that exchange. I like knowing her only as Gray Turner, investor and new guy in town. So I zone out from the rest of what Hunt drolls on about and look down the rows of evergreens, pines, and spruces.

As soon as I see her hat and that red jacket, I feel relieved, and it makes me smile.

Midge walks past at the same time as Hunt shouts in my ear. Ignoring him, I hear her say, "There it is again. Whatever has you happy, Gray Turner, you should keep it."

In my ear, Hunt says, "And do me a favor, Gray. Steer clear of women who have the power to destroy you like that again. I'm getting too old for this shit."

"You're forty-two," I counter.

But what he says lingers, knocking sense back into me with the reality that I'm not here for this. This isn't the time to develop feelings for a woman. I know better.

"Yeah, stop reminding me." I hear some shuffling on his end, and then he says, "I'll get you something good, Gray. You're a fucking Hall of Fame candidate. This shit will die down."

It doesn't feel like it, and right now I'm out here flirting with a girl who absolutely has no business getting wrapped up in my shit existence. I shift my stance wider, moving my weight to my better side, and look up to see Aurora holding on to West's arm while she laughs so hard that her eyes squeeze tight and she bends forward.

What's so fucking funny, West? I bite down on my back molars, trying to get it together. I wouldn't mind being the one pulling a laugh out of her like that. I don't know that I've ever made anyone laugh like that, if I'm being honest with myself.

"You hearin' me, Gray?" Hunt barks out, reminding me he's still there.

"I hear you," I tell him as I rake my eyes down the

blonde little thing I can't seem to stop looking at. And I heard what he said about steering clear, but he's not seeing things from my current point of view. I should ignore it. I should walk away from the only woman who's caught my attention in a long fucking time. But all I can think about is how *that's* what I want.

CHAPTER 4

AURORA

"There's sap everywhere."

Gray grumbles from under the tree, "West, you better fucking hold it."

"I'm holding it. My hands are going to be sticky for a week, but I'm holding it."

"Do you want to switch off?" I ask.

"Don't you dare fucking say yes, West."

I bite back my smile.

West lets go and walks over to me, saying quietly, "I don't know what exactly I walked in on last night, but he's actually been nicer this morning. So whatever it was, I approve. I caught him smiling without me having to crack a joke at my own expense."

"I'll keep that in mind." I like the idea that he was as affected as I was, and as much as I know I shouldn't be so fast to saddle up with someone, I want to. Tash said there are more people coming, to keep an open mind, but there's something about Gray that warms every bone in my body. He's not even here for the Winter Solstice. That should be my first indicator to rein in these thoughts, take a few steps away, and stop putting my hands on him, but I'm finding it impossible. I'm drawn to him. In a way I can't even begin to explain.

"Shouldn't you be—"

Before I can finish the thought, the tree falls over, and with it, a succession of *fucks* and *shits* come piling out of both of their mouths. West rushes over and Gray pulls himself up from the ground.

"I thought at least one of you was holding it," Gray deadpans.

I have to roll my lips to hide my giggle wanting to escape, scrunching my nose. "Sorry, I got distracted." There's only amusement coating his features as he looks at me. Walking over to him, I brush off the pine needles that are stuck to his cheek and the dirty snow from his arm.

But the cackling that passes us quickly distracts me. With a glare I really don't deserve, two sets of couples walk past. Two fishermen I met last summer at the Lobster Festival, and the women they're now engaged to. I didn't know who they were or, more importantly, that they were with anybody, but I kissed them both. Only to find out they had been in long-term relationships. To be fair, maybe kissing is a little too vague for what it was. I kissed one of them on the lips, and the other made out with my southern pair. It was the Summer Solstice, a full moon, and I was feeling myself. The attention had me saying yes to all of it. I hadn't known they were meant for other people.

Come to find out, one of them had a diamond ring in his pocket, ready to propose when they docked. But in truth to how people can really suck sometimes, it turns out it's my fault they're pigs. At least, according to the two women who like to make nasty comments whenever I'm within earshot. Tash knows all about it. Gossip moves faster than the tides around here. I've witnessed Tash deal with it through the majority of my teenage years. And she'd simply roll her eyes and wink at me.

"She's just so trashy. I mean, look at what she's wearing," the one with the shiny puffer coat says. And really, I shouldn't take their opinions to heart, but I do. I'm an empath. So, as much as it stings to hear her words, I know she's just hurt. I apologized when I realized what had happened. I thought the fishermen were single. How could I have known they were with anyone? They hadn't said they were. They didn't have rings on, and they flirted right back. Not to mention, they put their mouths where they didn't belong.

The other one, a woman I had bought flowers from often at Wild Tide's flower shop, mumbles, "Didn't think you'd end up being one of those women. Homewrecker." And then eyes Tash, mouthing, "Witch."

I wipe my cheek, batting away the tear that's

stupidly escaped. I never let them get to me like this. But the fact that Gray is witnessing this makes it worse.

The deep timbre of Gray's voice rolls through me, his warm palm splayed across the small of my back when he says loudly, "Hey, guy."

They all stop. Both men look at him.

The taller of the two, Daryl, responds. Or maybe it was Darren; I can't even remember now. "Oh shit, you're Gray Turner. I heard you moved up this way."

But Gray disregards that. "I'd rather not tell two women to shut their fucking mouths on such a nice day, but I'll do it if I hear one more nasty comment slung at her." He nudges his head toward me, so it's clear who he's talking about.

One drops the wreaths they are carrying while the other stands and watches like he just got caught out all over again.

West steps forward, arms out, trying to diffuse the elevated voices and attitudes.

But Gray isn't done. "I'd suggest you four move the fuck along. There's nothing much uglier than grown-ass women saying shitty things to someone. And you two"—he points at the two men—"if you got something to say, I got nothing but a shitty reputation to uphold."

I look down and try to suppress my poorly timed smile because a few shouts and swears follow. And I'll be honest, I've never wanted to climb a person more in my entire life.

Tash cuts in and says, "When you girls figure out

what's wrong with this situation, you come to see me, and we'll get you matched properly."

And that's Tash. Even after hearing closed minds, she still wants to help people find who might make them happy. She winks at me. "They don't know where to put their anger. They'll figure it out soon enough."

Gray moves next to me once they start walking away, his mouth at my ear as he says, "Don't give a fuck what might have happened there, but nobody talks to you like that. You hear me?"

The way he says it like it's the rule now has me instantly relaxing, breathing in a way that makes it seem like I hadn't been exhaling fully until this very moment.

Yeah, I hear you.

I can't stop from staring into those hazel eyes of his. They're searching mine like he needs to see I'm not upset any longer or, at the very least, distracted. And I definitely am. "Thank you," I tell him softly, moving in closer, just for him to hear.

He hooks his pinky with mine. A small move that nobody would notice, but it makes me feel like he's got me. A friend. A protector. A carefulness I haven't felt before.

His eyes shift down, staring at my lips, and I never would have categorized myself as a strong woman. Kind and resilient, sometimes crass, but never having the kind of strength and willpower I'm exercising as I hold myself back from kissing him. Tasting his bold words and confidence with my tongue. Regardless of who he might be or whomever else I might be intended for.

"You better stop looking at me like that, Aurora."

A wide smile takes over my face, and I watch his pupils dilate as he takes it in. I know exactly what I'm doing, and I couldn't stop it even if I tried. "How am I looking at you?"

His throat bobs as he swallows. This gruff, tough guy feels like he'd melt right into me if I wrapped my arms and legs around him.

"Like you'd take me so fucking well."

So. Turned. On.

Goosebumps fly up my arms, underneath my layers. Tingles all the way down my neck and back, swooping over my ass and right up to my core. I open my mouth to tell him yes. Yes, I would. But a cold wind dances around us at the same time that the horn of my truck beeps, knocking away the question and the answer I'm so eager to give.

Gray pulls away, and I hate it. I'd rather have him pressed close, whispering anything he wants, just for me. But he surprises me again when he pulls up our hooked fingers and brushes a kiss against my wrist. "Let's go, Trouble."

I shiver. His lips anywhere near my skin shake me awake in the best way. "I'm not trouble. I'm delightful."

He leads me in front of him. As his hand moves to my lower back, he leans into my neck. "Oh honey, you're absolutely every single kind of trouble for me."

Our lighthouse lamps spin at their programmed times, shining across the smokey ocean. The windows from the main room in the lighthouse are the best seats in town to watch storms roll in from the water view. I couldn't imagine being on a boat out there at this time of night, in the cold. I used to think that might be where *he* was coming from. I used to imagine all types of ways I'd meet my person. My partner. My family.

Tash was that for me. And I would have been okay with that, but she told me I would find the person who would fill me with so much love that I'd feel it in my soul.

When a matchmaker tells you the month and year that your life will change, it's not the kind of information you just forget about. Since I was sixteen, I knew he would come. I would stand on the bluffs in the summer, and inside the lighthouse in the winter, watching for boats to come into the harbor. Thinking he might be on one. I knew everyone in town; tourists would become regulars, and I never wanted to leave. I was content with working and not leaving for college or university. Tash allowed me to make those decisions about my own life. And Wild Tide was my home. But he wasn't here. At least not before.

"Now *that's* a fucking tree," West barks out, hands on his hips, surveying the last few hours of decorating we put into it.

I like him. The way he's light and eager to make the

people around him smile. But he's not the Turner brother who keeps making my pulse beat faster with every glance.

"He's a good guy," West says quietly next to me.

"Seems like it," I say with a measured tone as I review my list. I need to make sure I've remembered everything I wanted to hang on the tree and the mantle in the main room.

"The best guy I know. But I guess you could say I'm biased."

Smiling at him, I can see how much he loves his brother. "Maybe a little." I look down at his hand as he massages the palm of his other. "Can I take a look?"

His eyebrows shoot up, questioning what I mean.

"I can get an idea about things–a bird's eye view."

He moves his hand toward me, palm side up, and I drag my fingers along the heart and head lines that are deep and arched.

"Is this what people mean when they say you and Tash are witchy?"

"Is that what they're saying lately?"

"I don't like to repeat rumors, but people talk. Small town, I kind of expected it." He watches as I trace my fingers along the lines of his palms. "So Tash is the matchmaker and you're, what? Some kind of fortune teller, then?"

I flick my eyes up to his. "You should talk to Tash about those rumors. But for me, I like to study palms. One of our friends who comes in for the Winter Solstice taught me." I drag my finger along his heart line, and while there is something to be said for the lust and romance that exist along its deep shape, I'm more interested in looking at the aspects that aren't as obvious. Find out if I'm seeing this correctly.

"You're a creative," I observe, looking up at him. "But it's not traditional like painting or drawing." I think through what I'm seeing a bit, the curve of the lines and how they intersect. "Not writing. Is it food?"

"You can see that there?" West asks with a bit of awe, staring at the lines I'm studying along his wrist and above his thumb. "The creative piece, yes, the food part was an assumption that you just confirmed." I wink and give him a smirk. I can see even more, but I don't like to dive too deep until I've read a person a few times. I move my focus toward the mounts beneath his thumb.

He laughs and says, "Are you a bullshitter, Aurora? Usually, I can spot my own kind." That makes me chuckle.

"I'm a lot of things, unfortunately that's not one of them. I can't tell your future, but I can say that you thrive when you have a purpose. Your family will grow, but just like most things, you need to put down roots first."

Before I can finish, Gray yells, "West." We both look over, and he doesn't look happy. In fact, he looks like he could knock his brother out if West gives him a decent reason. Gray glances down at how I'm holding West's hand, his jaw clenching so hard I can see the muscles tick in his neck as he looks back up at me. "West, I need you over here."

West pulls his hand from mine and smiles. Under his breath, he says, "Someone's jealous."

"Now," Gray barks out, gruff and short. It's a demand, and even though he's not talking to me, *goddesses*, do I feel it.

CHAPTER 5

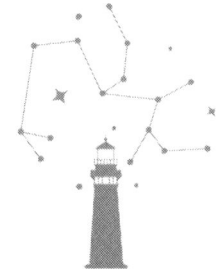

GRAY

"Pint or a pitcher, handsome?" the waitress practically shouts in my face. She smacks gum around her mouth as she pours beer, waiting for my response.

Looking over to see what's on tap, there's nothing listed on the handles, so I decide on a safe bet. "How about a Guinness?"

She smirks and moves down the counter to deliver a fresh pie that just dinged out from the kitchen window behind her.

"Mind if I join you, Mr. Turner?" a familiar sweet voice says to my left. Aurora smiles, leaning over the counter to see past the man next to us. I don't know how I could have missed her when I walked in. As soon as my gaze lands on her, it has a hard time looking anywhere else. Her blonde curls are pulled up in a chaotic knot on the top of her head, lips shiny from the slice of pizza she's just bit into, eyes sparkling with playfulness.

The older man sitting between us stares ahead at the hockey game playing above the bar. Aurora turns her smile to him. "Mr. Napolitano, do you mind swapping seats with me? I'd like to sit with my friend."

A simple request, but I more than like how it sounds. I haven't had one of those in a while. A friend. Someone other than my brother. And while I'm still unclear what the hell happened between this woman and me in the kitchen the other night, I'll take the title of friend for now.

Mr. Napolitano turns his head and sizes me up. "Sure thing, Aurora." When he stands, he leans into my space. "You're the best player Boston ever had—at least while I've been alive—and I'm circling close eight decades now. I wouldn't mind you joining some of us down at the VA if you're ever interested in talking baseball."

It's an invite I never knew I wanted until this very moment. "Thank you, sir." I give him a tight-lipped nod as he slides down a seat. "I'll take you up on that sometime."

"Those guys will go nuts if you show up," Aurora says, taking a sip of her drink.

Feeling a bit lighter than when I walked in a few minutes ago, I tease her, "So we're friends, hmm?"

She looks over her shoulder at the restaurant that's buzzing behind us. "It's Friday night, Gray, which means it's pizza and beer night. I'm friends with every single person who wants to have a PBR and slice with me." With a glance around my face, she smiles coyly. "Even if I've had their fingers and tongue in my mouth."

Just the mention of it makes my gut do a fucking backflip. Changing the subject faster than my head can keep up with, she nods to the pitcher the waitress is pouring. "Are we polishing off this pitcher together?"

I clear my throat. "Um..." I fumble for anything that sounds like words. "I ordered a Guinness, but—" Like she's answering the question for me, the waitress puts down the same sized glass that Aurora's sipping from, filled to the brim with a light golden beer.

"Handsome, we only serve Blue Ribbon, Wild Tide tap water, and the best goddamn pizza you've ever tasted here," she says between chomps of that gum.

Aurora smiles into her glass when I look over to her. She inches closer once the waitress moves on, and the moment she does, my body preens with awareness. Chest warming, the brush of her arm against mine is a place I'll keep connected for as long as she'll allow. And I won't even talk about how my cock just punched my leg. It was already stirring the minute she said something about her mouth. I stare back down at those lips of hers.

Jesus, I have barely any self-control, and I'm in the middle of a crowded family restaurant.

"Pia only has two volumes: shouting and yelling. I promise, it's not you." Leaning up on her chair, she grabs a stack of napkins from behind the counter. I take in her worn sweatshirt that's been cut at the neckline. It falls slightly off her shoulder where a black bra strap peeks out in its place. My eyes travel down to her black leggings, that I'm pretty confident have nothing underneath. There's not an underwear line in sight, only the curve of her ass and a little slice of skin where her shirt creeps up. When she sits back on the stool, she takes a slice of pizza from the pie in front of her and plops it on my plate.

I take a bite and raise my eyebrows.

She knows right away what I'm thinking. "Best pizza, right?"

"It's good." I wipe my mouth. "Have you ever tried the pizza in New Hav—"

"Bah bah bah," she mumbles out loudly, putting her hand over my mouth. "Don't let anyone hear you say that, Gray," she adds in a whisper-shout, with a quick shake of her head. "We don't speak of other pizzerias when we're at Bozzy's."

It's impossible not to laugh as she shifts her eyes around, genuinely concerned that someone may have heard me. As she pulls her hand away from my mouth and smiles, a flush creeps up from her neck and onto her cheeks. Her hand just pressed over my mouth has me thinking about all the places I'd like to drag my lips. This woman is goddamn enchanting. She takes a big bite of her cheese pizza and widens her eyes at me, humming in approval that I match. I can't remember the last time it was this easy to smile back at someone.

A loud echo of laughter kicks in behind us, and it knocks me out of whatever trance that entire exchange just put me in. The restaurant space is small, but stacked with at least a dozen round tables, all filled with people eating and drinking. I had just wrapped up with the architect for the downtown businesses when I saw the neon lit sign for Bozzy's Pizzeria. Normally, a packed restaurant isn't appealing to me, but it looked inviting, and smelled damn good too. That sweet smell of bread and the saltiness of melted cheeses had my mouth watering before I stepped inside.

Sitting here now, with a hockey game on the big screens and families eating together in the background, I like being in the mix of it. When I look over at Aurora demolishing another slice, it feels like something I could get used to doing.

"You do this every Friday night, pizza and beer...by yourself?"

Before I can stare too long at the grease lining her plush lips, she wipes it, saying, "It's the best Friday night plans I've ever had, so why mess with a good thing?" I like how that sounds. The idea of enjoying something so simple and doing it for no other reason or motive than to end the week with some pizza and beer. My routines have always been about pre-made meals, working out, and improving my game. Doing more, more, more, with my eye on the prize. Tack that on to not being able to wander into a place like this back in Boston without being heckled and photographed. A Friday night like this was never an option in the life I was living.

"Sometimes Tash will come with me, but usually I just hang out with whomever is saddled up at the bar." She pours out more beer from her pitcher into both of our glasses. "I've been doing it since high school." She smiles innocently, taking a sip. "The pizza part, not the beer."

"What was it like growing up here?"

She pulls at a piece of cheese hanging from her new slice. I know what it looks like when you're trying to frame an answer for the listener's benefit versus sharing a truth. But then she surprises me. "There were good days and hard days. I've always been more focused on the good days, but it's the hard ones that taught me something. It wasn't always the easiest having a unique upbringing. Tash adopted me when I was just a baby." She clears her throat. "Fun fact: I was born in Iceland."

I didn't expect her to pivot so quickly, but now I'm interested in whatever she wants to share with me. "How did you end up here?"

"My mama knew Tash when they were young. They grew up together, their mothers were friends." She shifts her body closer, and I do the same without even realizing, now both facing each other, opposite elbows leaning on the counter. "There wasn't a father listed on my birth certificate. And my mother passed away two days after having me. Internal bleeding they weren't able to fix. But she was alive long enough to make sure I was okay. She called Tash from the hospital, and then I ended up on a plane back to Wild Tide with Tash a few months later." She wipes the corner of her eye, keeping a tear from escaping. "Most of this I didn't know until I was older. At that point in her life, Tash hadn't known what was going on with my mother. She wasn't sure who my father could be, but she knew that she wanted me."

This time, her smile feels less genuine than the rest I've seen her give. "Growing up here, being here now, it's where I'm supposed to be. I truly believe that. And most days are great. Wild Tide has a way of digging into you, kind of like the way cold rolls off the ocean or when the holidays approach. Your body remembers it. The way it makes you feel."

"Fenway," I say in response.

"Fenway?" she repeats, her eyes finding mine. "The baseball stadium?"

I wipe my mouth with a stack of the thin paper napkin squares. "The feeling I get every time I walk from Yawkey Way into the park. Whether it was as just a fan when I was younger, or later as a player, it didn't matter. It always gave me that same feeling." I can't help but grin at the thought of it.

She tilts her head. "Home?"

"Home," I exhale. I take all of her in for the briefest moment, the tiny diamond in her nose that mingles with the few freckles across the bridge. The way her eyes seem to be a new shade of green and gold right now. Deeper and warmer. Her rosy cheeks and matching lips.

"Maybe you can show me your version of home sometime," she says, breaking my study of her every feature. One eye squints shut, her voice lowering to a whisper like she's about to make a confession. "I've never been to a major league game." My eyes widen, sitting taller, and she holds up her hands, laughing at my reaction. "I don't think I've ever been to Boston either, now that I think about it. There was a class trip when I was in sixth grade, but I didn't go."

If I hadn't already experienced the way her laugh ignited every part of me, I definitely feel it now. Somehow melting the edges and gliding right into the parts of me that I'd shut down. I can't keep the smirk off my face when I make her a promise. "Yeah, I'll take you sometime." It's the kind of promise I mean too, not just a thing to say in the moment.

I settle up the bill when she excuses herself to the bathroom.

When we step out front, zipping up jackets and exhaling visible puffs of air, I try to come up with an excuse to keep this impromptu date from ending.

"Thank you for dinner, by the way. It was nice to have some company," she says, pulling on a pair of earmuffs.

"I like your kind of company."

She looks up at the sky and smiles, waiting for a beat before tilting her head back to me. "Are you in a rush to get back, or..."

"I don't have anywhere to be," I reply before she can even finish. When I go to ask her where to next, she's smirking at me like I've missed what's amusing.

"Do me a favor, Mr. Turner. Don't wear a baseball hat around me."

My brows furrow as she starts walking down the

main drag of downtown Wild Tide. When just a few of my strides catch up next to her, I have to laugh. "Why's that?"

Looking at my hat, she drags her gaze down the rest of me, lingering for just a moment longer on my lap and back up again. I won't lie, Aurora blatantly checking me out makes me feel really fucking good. And plenty of women have done it. Women asking for what they want and being direct isn't anything new, but from her, it feels entirely original.

"You have to know what you look like. I mean...it's a wow." Laughing lightly, her eyes go wide. "But with a hat on, it's..." She shakes her head, biting the inside of her lip as she thinks for a moment. "I don't think I'll be able to form words if you're wearing a backwards baseball hat."

"Good to know, baseball hat equals silence if I should ever need it." Not that I'd want her quiet. I like listening to her talk about her life, this place. It keeps my attention on the here and now and out of my head.

"You picked a good night to wander downtown, actually," she says. When we turn the corner, and I see the street lined with people and vendors overlooking the docks, I understand why. "It's Light the Harbor tonight."

Sailboats are anchored out in a long line from the harbor to a decent way out to shore. You can see the lighthouse at The Timekeeper in the distance, lit with both its spinning beacon and the Christmas lights strung up along the edges of the windows and walkway. She leads us down the stairs to the docks and explains, "Most towns light one big tree in their downtown area, but we like to decorate the harbor." A loud foghorn from a tow boat sounds off, and the trio that had been playing when we walked up starts again, this time a folk-like version of *Winter Wonderland*. "And the ocean."

When I follow her line of sight, I see buoys illuminated with red and green lights, and at the farthest one, there's a small boat tied to it with white lights. The Christmas tree that sits inside twinkles with color and a shiny gold star at the top. It moves back and forth like a metronome, following whatever pattern the water intends. It's freezing down here, the wind never taking a break. A constant reminder that the ocean is a few feet away and winter has arrived, but on these docks, it has a nastier bite to it. We stand off the side and listen to an accordion lead as the harmonica player and guitarist try to keep up. I blow into my hands to keep them warm.

"Here," she says, grabbing on to one of my hands and lacing her fingers with mine. She tucks our clasped hands into her coat pocket and moves us to the other side of the dock and right in front of a small drink cart. I swear within moments, I absorb her warmth. "This is the only reason I ever come here. The lights are pretty and all, but this sipping chocolate is the most delicious thing you'll ever put in your mouth."

The second she says it, she smiles, because we both know that's not true. I look down at her lips. "I doubt that." Then I watch as her cheeks turn pink. With her hand still wrapped around mine, I give it a squeeze. *Dammit, I like her.*

"Aurora," the woman behind the cart practically shrieks as we step up. The cart is simple, with an oversized pot that looks like it's being churned. Alongside it is a small stack of cups and lids. The sign below reads Whip & Drizzle, and the young girl manning it looked like she hated her life until she saw Aurora step up. I get it. "I saved a shot of raspberry sauce for you."

"Yes," she whisper-shouts. "This is my friend, Gray," she says, beaming up at me. "Gray, this is my friend, Luna, the best chocolatier and pâtissier you'll ever meet."

"She's not wrong." Luna smiles as she ladles out a thick, dark sauce into a tumbler. Then I watch as she steams it, dropping some combination of cinnamon sticks and star-shaped spices into the metal cup. "I don't have any more raspberry sauce for you, Gray, but I can do a dash of orange, or maybe a peppermint?"

I raise my free hand. "I'm still full from pizza."

"You sure, Gray? Luna only makes her grandmother's sipping chocolate once a year, and this is it." She leans in closer to me and whispers, "I'm not sharing if you change your mind, Mr. Turner."

Why does that hit me right in the cock every time she says it?

I watch as Luna gives her a smirk.

"I'm sure."

She points at her friend. "Luna, if there's any left, I'll take it."

"Deal. Although, there's a big turnout this year. More than usual, just like Tash mentioned." When she smiles, it's like they share another wordless exchange. "It's December."

Aurora sips and replies, "It's December."

Luna shifts her eyes to me.

"Hey, you two can gab anytime," Midge Parrish yells from behind us. "It's freezing down here. Move it along, Luna."

Luna rolls her eyes. "Talk to you soon, love. Gray, it was nice to meet you."

As we move along, Midge says, "I thought that was you, Gray Turner. Smiling again, I see."

When we're up the stairs from the docks, I stop and have to ask, "What's so special about December?" She keeps walking, but our linked fingers inside her jacket anchor her to me. I don't want to let go.

Glancing above my head, then back at me, she smirks.

"Good?" I ask, looking at the espresso cup as she takes another sip.

"One of the most delicious things I've ever tasted."

"Let me have a taste," I say, deeper than intended.

She shakes her cup, showing me it's empty. Then she shifts her eyes above my head again. Following her line of sight, there's a bundle of greens with white berries the size of a fist strung up between the light posts. Mistletoe. When our eyes meet, she smiles at me, waiting for my move. I pull our clasped hand that's been resting in her coat pocket to tug her closer, eclipsing the light between us.

"It's bad luck to ignore Mistletoe," she says in a

whisper just seconds before I crash my lips against hers. Every part of me can't get enough of this woman. From the tips of the fingers that are still grasping hers to the tip of my tongue that's being massaged in a way I've been craving since the first time I laid eyes on her. She tastes like the spiked chocolate she just sipped. Decadent and sweet. A twinge of raspberry with the warm tang of licorice.

It's the few claps and whistles that knock me back into reality. Before I'm able to pull away from her, she fists her free hand in the material of my coat. I may tower over her, but the little thing pulls me closer as she whispers, "Delicious, right?"

With her lips still ghosting over mine, my eyes flick to the hoots and whistles. With camera phones held up, it's pretty clear this has quickly become a spectacle, and I panic. I drop her hand and step away from her. *This was careless.*

Two people walk toward me and start asking, "Gray Turner, oh my gosh. Can we..." But I don't listen for the rest. I know it's a bad look, but I have no interest in being a social media post and tag, just to have this moment with Aurora dissected and discussed. I don't even know what I'm doing. How would I even begin to explain it?

"I need to get out of here," I tell her.

Her eyebrows furrow, her concern making me want nothing more than to go right back to that kiss. "It's fine, Gray. I'll walk with–"

"No," I bite back, rougher than I wanted, but I need to get out of this situation. Alone. I don't look back. I don't want to see hurt or anger in those pretty hazel eyes. I fucking hate myself for making her wince at my words or think she did anything wrong. I'm the fuck-up here.

My phone buzzes in my pocket, and I see Hunt's already texting me.

Fucking hell.

CHAPTER 6

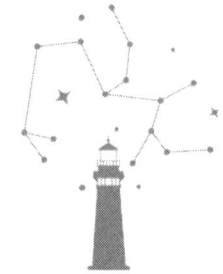

GRAY

> **HUNT**
> I saw a picture of you at a Tree Farm with a caption that said, 'Turner likes to make women cry at Christmas.'

> **GRAY**
> Are you shitting me?

> **HUNT**
> You still haven't answered me about the one I saw last night...
>
> Who is she?

> **GRAY**
> None of your business.

I don't want to know what picture it could have been, or how it was misconstrued, but the last thing I want is to have Aurora mixed into any of my bullshit.

This place is supposed to be my escape, not a news story.

> **HUNT**
> How do you feel about New York?

After last night, honestly, I was really liking *not* having options.

> **GRAY**
> It depends.

> **HUNT**
> I can work with that. Sit tight.

I zone out, staring at the ocean lit bright with the full moon suspended above it. It's too bright for stars, but at least it's not snowing. I spent most of the day today working through the less appealing side of renovations—balancing a budget with the unexpected things that have come up. Specifically, the very large colony of mice that had taken residence in the lot of buildings we've started gutting. Add that to the infrastructure issues rostered out for me yesterday when I met with our architect, and I'm feeling anxious about not being here for the entirety of the renovations. I ignore the fact that I ran away from Aurora last night. *Fucking asshole.* I haven't been able to find my balls that apparently retreated into my body since. I don't think starting something with her, however light or heavy it might be, is a good idea, but she didn't deserve my frustration. I owe her an apology.

Flipping up the collar of my jacket, I stuff my hands

into my pockets. I can't keep grinding my teeth like this, I'm going to crack something.

Just breathe. With a deep inhale, I watch the sailboats on the water glow with Christmas lights. And on the exhale, I focus on the way they glide along with whatever tide is coming in or going out. That Christmas tree in the rowboat lolls from a different angle tonight.

I liked the view better with her. Watching the boats in the harbor, with her. I haven't walked and talked with someone like that in a long time. I don't want to like it as much as I did. I tighten my fists in my pockets.

The ding from the buoy offshore makes me think that it'd be nice to have a boat here. I'm so all over the place that I instantly shake my head at the wandering idea. I unclench my fists and remind myself again that this isn't permanent. I'm not staying here. I weigh the thought of being here just for a season. I'll have to check on properties. But that doesn't sound right either. The idea of seeing Aurora with whomever she ends up with sounds like a punishment. And she'll end up with someone, because a woman like her won't be alone for long. She's the kind of woman who smart men don't pass up.

I close my eyes tight. Regardless of what Hunt warned me about, I shouldn't want someone so quickly, and so intensely. Especially after so long of not even wanting to look at a woman.

I tilt my neck back and peer up at the stars peppered along the deep navy sky. The way they linger there, bright and with just enough sparkle, they remind me of that little diamond nestled in the curve of Aurora's nose. *Fuck me.*

How am I supposed to forget about how it feels to kiss her? Or how she drags her nails along the back of my neck and up into my hair when our tongues collide. I have no business wanting this, wanting her, but I do–almost desperately. It's why I'm practically dancing outside of this lighthouse door.

My phone buzzes. My hand already clutched around it in my pocket.

WEST
Why are you pissed at me?

GRAY
I'm not.

WEST
Then why are you stomping around outside?

When I turn and look back at the Inn, I see West peering out from the kitchen window. I love my brother, but sometimes I feel guilty for dragging him places with me. He deserves his own life. He was doing well in Boston. There wasn't a restaurant opportunity yet, but he was establishing himself with private clients. I went ahead and had an entire life crisis, and he dropped his own life to figure things out with me. I need to be nicer to him.

Since I watched Aurora hold his hand, I've barely given my brother more than a few words. I know he doesn't deserve it. He told me she was reading his palm, but I still didn't like it. And as much as the cool air feels good, it's been long enough, weighing whether it's still a good idea to knock on that lighthouse door.

> **WEST**
> Listen, she grabbed my palm. I told you that already. And as cute as she is, she's only ever looking at you, brother.

> **GRAY**
> Is that right?

I know he's right. I know I'm the reason I'm not already half devouring that beautiful mouth of hers.

> **WEST**
> You know it is. Now, please stop stalling and just go knock on that door.

Snorting a laugh, I pocket my phone and walk back along the path that connects the Inn's side door to the lighthouse. It looks like it's balancing along the rocky ledge, but the wind isn't strong enough to snuff it out or knock it down. I'm starting to understand why my parents liked it here. There's something about Wild Tide and this inn that feels comfortable.

Once I'm standing in front of it, the door to the lighthouse swings open, and Aurora stands there with a warm, yellow hued light at her back. Arms crossed in front of her, she's already smiling when she asks, "Want to come inside?"

Fuck, she's beautiful.

I nod and step through the threshold, and I'm instantly hit with the warmth from the fireplace that's lit in the center of the room. "You were out there for a while. I thought you might have lost your nerve to knock."

"Needed to clear my head a little bit."

"Did you?" she asks as the heavy door closes behind us.

The walls are decorated with tapestries, some with intricate designs and soft-looking textures and others in solid colors like dark greens, deep reds, and different shades of purple. Small white Christmas lights highlight her mantle, along with candlesticks of various heights. Based on its size, a couch or even a mattress is against the farthest wall. Blankets and far too many pillows to count scattered across it. I don't know much about her, but if a room could *feel* like a person, this one feels like her.

I give her a clipped nod in response.

There's a plethora of beads separated by color in bowls around her desk with pliers and string. A sewing machine sits in the far corner and stacks of squares piled around it. Along with a small cart are black tins and brown twine with clipped herbs and dried flowers, too many to identify. At first glance, it looks like a stylish mess, but when I focus on each space, they're works in progress to the many things I'm realizing Aurora creates.

"I'm sorry," I say, searching her eyes, hoping she can see how much I mean it. I hate the way I spoke to her last night. I would have probably had words with anyone who would have done the same.

Her eyebrows raise, maybe not expecting the apology. "I know." The corner of her mouth tilts up, and it's the sweetest little twitch before she adds, "Last time I'll allow it, Mr. Turner."

And that breaks the tension and pulls a tight-lipped smile from my lips.

My eyes shift around the room again. "You have a lot of books." Full bookshelves line the wall, the overflow stacked on any available surface except her workbench. An oversized book lays open on a page of a star map, marked with tabs and notes along the margins in cursive handwriting. There are number charts I don't know much about and cards with faces and words instead of numbers and suits laid out in what looks like a special arrangement.

"I do," she says, following my movements as I take everything in. "Like what you see?"

The question has me turning to face her, dragging my eyes down the front of her body. Her loose and thick sweatpants might be baggy, but I like how they make her hips and ass curve and appear even fuller. I think about how warm her skin must feel underneath and how much I want to touch more of her. I stare at the smallest strip of skin that peeks out between her waistband and cropped shirt. The black sweater scoops low enough that her cleavage offers a mouthwatering view of the full tits and pebbled nipples beneath.

"I do." I swallow, suddenly eager to taste whatever she's willing to give me. "Very much. Maybe more than I should."

She smiles and leans against a chair, perching on its edge.

"That's the sky right now, this time of year and in this hemisphere." She nods to the opened star map. "Do you want to see?"

I'm not quite sure how anybody tells her no to something she wants—I'm not sure I could. Everything about this feels like I'm exactly where I'm supposed to be. I'm leaning into a feeling, ignoring that voice in the back of my head warning me to not get attached. "Show me," I say, my voice much grittier than expected.

She bites her bottom lip and pauses a second before standing. I follow as she walks up the metal spiral staircase that's just behind her workspace. "Be prepared, Gray. This is the best view in all of Wild Tide."

"Already is," I mutter under my breath.

And while I meant the view of her beautiful face, I can't help but stare as her peachy ass ticks back and forth as we climb the stairs. When we reach the top, I have to force myself to look away. I'm greeted by windows all around—all the way to the ceiling. Ten or so more steps up to the top level is the massive light that spins and whirls, creating a guide for whomever might need it on the water. The round space isn't large, but enough of a landing to be able to walk around the entire perimeter and even sit to look out.

"It's a clear night, too. You lucked out," she says as she kneels in front of the windows, facing away from the ocean and toward where the Inn sits on the expansive dark property below. "December can be tricky."

"I couldn't see this many stars earlier. The moon was too bright." Looking out over the ocean, the horizon line clearly defines where the water meets the sky. I settle into the feeling that everything seems so inconsequential from this view, and it's like I can breathe a bit deeper.

She interrupts my stare. "The water and the sky are beautiful together, but this is what's truly incredible." All along the window ledges in front of where she sits are odds and ends, crystals and dried herbs, a set of binoculars, a compass, and a protractor.

"There's something special about The Timekeeper Inn, don't you think?" Her tone is suggestive, like she's going to tell me more, and honestly, I'm hanging on to her every word. I'm eager to listen to her opinions and discoveries. Being near someone excited about a hobby or new idea is contagious.

"Something," I say as I study her. Then more quietly to myself, "Someone." My arm brushes hers as I sit next to her, tingling at the contact. It feels good to be close to her again.

"Okay, so bear with me here," she says excitedly, clearing her throat. "I'm going to show you something that makes absolutely no sense." Leaning into me, she points out to the sky, almost straight ahead, slightly moving her finger up and down. "Do you see that bright star? The one just above the roof of the main house?"

With my line of sight, I follow to where she's pointing. "I think so." I stretch out my bad knee and sit almost so I'm facing her while she looks out the windows. There's nothing like sitting on the floor as you creep toward your forties to really drive home the notion of aging. It's the first time today I've thought about it, though.

"Your knee okay?" she asks thoughtfully.

I tilt my head and brush it off. "It's fine."

"You have the brooding thing down, but you're not a very good liar." She smiles, quirking a brow at me. "I made you something for it."

Before I can thank her, she points out against the glass. "Okay, now look up just a little to another star right above the other."

She moves in even closer, and the way she smells like cinnamon and something sweet has me closing my eyes on an inhale. It would be so easy to brush my lips along her collarbone, the space where her neck meets her chest, just before the scoop of that sweater.

"That would be the pendulum. If you could imagine a clock, that's the shape." Reaching over me, she grabs a small handheld flashlight and flicks it on. It casts a blue light against the glass window, illuminating a drawing that wasn't there a second ago. It's a perfectly straight line between the two stars she just showed me and connects to a few more. "That constellation is called The Clock."

It's hard not to smile at the coincidence of it. "And it's right above The Timekeeper Inn."

"Exactly." She smiles, turning her head to look at me.

Her eyes shift to my mouth, and I can only think, *go ahead, baby girl, take a taste.*

"You can see it best around midnight. In December.

Which makes it beautifully timed. But the most unbelievable part is that it's a southern hemisphere constellation. Which means we shouldn't be able to see it from here at all." She looks back out, tracing the drawing with her finger. "But there it is, in plain sight, right above my home."

"Our home." My correction has my throat tightening. *What the hell am I doing?*

My pulse has already been all over the place since I stepped foot in here. Slow and steady as I looked out on the horizon line, but fast and erratic with every move this woman makes. I don't understand what about her has me in a chokehold. I didn't think before I spoke. She knows the surface of those words—I partly own the place she calls home. But the underlying meaning that lingers has her shifting closer and slowly climbing into my lap. I let her. I watch her, eyes locked on me, as she settles into my lap as if she were a pet getting comfortable with its owner. And fuck do I want to own her right now. I wonder if she can feel how my body buzzes beneath her. My breaths shorten as all the blood rushes from my head to right below where she's perched.

"Why midnight?"

I brush the hair from her shoulders as she places her hands on my chest. I like her touching me. It's comforting, and I realize now how touch deprived I've been.

"Okay, stay with me on this, big guy." She smirks, and it's so damn cute. "I believe in things like stars and signs. Constellations and numbers. When mixed with herbs and intentions, the time of year and physical elements can shift moods and inspire important moments between people."

"Like this one?"

Her expression softens, but she doesn't answer. "That's how I like to look at the world. In layers, with meaning, and rarely at face value."

I'm at war with myself because I can't help but focus on her mouth. I want to kiss her, taste her tongue, and bite at her lips, but I'm caught up with what she's saying. I'm not sure if she's making the most sense of things I've never taken the time to understand, or if she's on the cusp of where quirky meets crazy. Either way, I'm captivated.

"Tash has always told me that midnights are for lovers. That break in time that turns night to day, giving love a fresh start. But I think maybe it's just that it's the darkest hour and you can see the brightness more clearly then."

I focus on where she's looking, but it's what she's saying that has me seeing something new. A completely different perspective than my own.

"I can't tell if I've completely lost you, or if you can't think past the hard-on nudging my ass." She smiles, lips pursing to the side, and I bark out a laugh.

"Sorry about that," I say, moving to lift her away from me. The last thing I want is for her to think I can't contain myself near her, like some fucking pervert.

She laughs with me as her hands move to my shoulders and loop around my neck. "I like exactly where I am." Her fingers drag along the base of my neck and into my hair. *Why does that feel so damn good?*

I don't think, just move, gripping her waist and hauling her flush against me. My hands smooth around her back, holding her close, as I look into the greens and golds of her hazel eyes. She doesn't pull away or try to take charge, only tightens her arms around my neck. Her mouth hovers just slightly above mine, waiting for my move, which I don't hesitate a second longer to make.

Pressing my palm into her back, I snake my arm up higher to tilt her head down, brushing my lips against hers. She hums as soon as we connect, and it ratchets up my pulse. I feel the kiss everywhere, along the edges of my skin, from the back of my neck to the tip of my cock, to every goosebump spreading down my arms. The way she melts into me, needing to be closer, sets me off. I can't help but groan at the way the seam of her lips part in perfect timing. The languid way her tongue caresses mine is so fucking sexy that I grip the edges of her shirt, grasping for anything to feel her closer. I need more of her.

"I like kissing you," she says sweetly, taking a small nip at my lip. And fuck, do I like kissing her too.

"You want to know what I'm thinking?" I mumble against her.

She hums in response, smiling against my mouth as her forehead rests on mine, before grazing her lips lightly over my beard. I want her to know that it's not just a physical attraction for me. It's all the parts of her that I'm discovering.

"I'm thinking that what you said makes a lot of sense. I don't know anything about stars and whatever it is you do out here, but I want to know more." I swipe my thumb along the edge of the sweater, and my knuckles brush the curve of her breast. My cock stirs beneath her, and she lets a small sound escape in response. *I've never wanted anyone the way I want her.* "There aren't many people who surprise me anymore. In a good way, at least." Her breathing picks up in pace with mine. "I can usually figure people out in the first few minutes of meeting them." I run my thumb along her chin, meeting her eyes. Pulling her closer, I hover in front of her lips and whisper, "Except for you."

She smiles, eyes lowering in a slow blink, like she's as affected as I am from the way we're wrapped up in each other. The dimple that puckers on her cheek as she bites at her bottom, kiss-swollen lip is her tell. Every time she's done it, I know exactly what she's thinking. What she wants. And thank fuck, that's me.

AURORA

I open my eyes and barely register the night sky in front of me. Every part of my body grows heated and eager for more as Gray tightens his arms around me. He licks and nips at my neck and then circles back, leaving kisses along the same line. I like how he holds me tightly, in the exact place he wants. There's something to be said about being in the arms of a strong man. I've never felt this wanted or secure in the arms of anyone. I'm damn near melting. With his hands wandering down below my ass, I grind against him.

He groans at the move. "That. Fuck, I need that," he says in his low, deep voice that reaches right between my legs. "Do it again, baby."

I smile. I like him calling me that. So I roll my hips again, this time harder, right along his cock that's lined up so nicely below me. My mouth parts and a small moan escapes at the feel of him. I'm not interested in overthinking. Only feeling.

"I haven't wanted," he pauses to kiss along my jawline, "anyone. This way."

"What way?" I ask breathily, needy for him to tell me more.

"In every way I shouldn't." He exhales slowly, maybe grounding himself or holding back. "Like I want to kiss you, taste you, fill you..."

Goddesses, he's perfect. "Can I be direct, then?"

He hums a yes as he leans into my neck, teasing the space just behind my ear. It sends a current through my entire body and lights up any remaining part of me that may have been slow to this delicious foreplay.

"I want you," I huff out. "I want you so badly, Gray."

Pulling back, his hand grips my chin. "Good. Stand up, baby."

I do what he asks, more than willing to follow his lead. He's not the kind of man I want to tease. I don't think I could handle the wait. As I stand above him, in between his legs, I watch as he raises his hands. With his eyes on me, he hooks his fingers into the waistband of my sweats, but he doesn't move any farther. He searches my eyes for approval to keep going.

"This okay?"

I exhale, "yes," smiling down at him. I help move my pants lower until they reach mid-thigh. He stops and leans in, kissing the top of each thigh, but when he pulls back, he smirks. My cropped top hides nothing. No panties.

"Get these off," he says as we both work to get my feet out of them.

I let out a giggle at his tone and eagerness.

The way he's looking at me, how it feels to hear him so turned on by my body, by talking passionately about the things that make me tick, it's a new high.

Reaching up, he glides his thumb along the seam of my pussy, the light touch almost making my knees buckle with anticipation. My muscles clench as he rubs around the arousal already slicked along my lips, almost releasing a whimper. "Fuck, look at you. I can't wait to taste you." He takes that same thumb and sucks it into his mouth. "So wet. So sweet."

I hum a response. It feels so good to be touched like this. I feel worshiped, and it fuels me with confidence I hadn't realized I lacked. I feel bolder, sexier.

"Tell me," I say, practically out of breath. I want him to tell me what he wants or what he wants me to do.

He's so tall, so big that it doesn't take much for him to sit up and lean into me, swiping his tongue along the same path his thumb just outlined. I gasp as he groans into me, the sound feels like a vibration. Pulling me closer, he kneads his hands into my ass. The squeeze is rough, but there's no other way I'd want it.

But instead of answering my demand with words, he leans back and smirks. His lips and chin shine with my arousal as he guides me down, leaning back into the pillows lining the floor. He pulls me up toward his head and it's clear he knows exactly what he wants from me. *Goddesses, do I want it too.*

"You want me to tell you to grind your needy little pussy all over my face?"

My lips tilt up, breaking into an approving smile. And on an exhale, I can't keep from moaning in response to his beautifully dirty mouth.

He rubs his nose along my clit as his lips and tongue drag up my slit.

"Or do you want me to tell you that I'd like your cum smeared all over my mouth and beard so I can smell you long after we've finished?"

"Goddesses." I tremble, rolling my hips forward, kneeling high.

Is it possible to be edged with words?

I gasp out as he nips at my clit. Looping his arms under my thighs, he pulls me right into his mouth. My entire weight on him, his tongue thrusts and his beard rubs exactly where I need. It feels better than any oral I've ever had. In fact, everything before this was a closed-mouth peck compared to the way his lips and tongue work me over thoroughly. He holds my thighs tight, and I do exactly as I'm told. Riding his face with abandon, I soak his beard and get lost in the way my body feels to be savored like this.

"Yesssssss..." I tilt my head back, barely seeing the night sky above or the revolving light at the top of the lighthouse. The undercurrent of everything I've been feeling when this man touches me comes to a crest, and as it falls over, crashing into me, my lips part to cry out. It's suddenly quiet, ringing in my ears, until I hear my own voice finishing with his name. "Gray," I moan as my chest shudders and thighs shake. I can't keep the smile off my lips as I come down from an orgasm that raked through every nerve ending within me.

I can barely hold my body up, but I don't have to. Gray lifts me enough to pull me down the front of his body. He's smiling as he kisses my forehead. "Good job, baby girl."

As I settle against his chest, I mumble, "I should be saying that to you." The rumble of his laugh is muffled against my ear. I listen to the beat in his chest, and it echoes so sweetly that my face hurts from the way I can't stop smiling.

It's a steady chime.

But then I hear it again. I open my eyes, blinking rapidly. As the third ring sounds, I sit up to make sure I'm hearing it. The fourth ring has me rising off of Gray. *Shit.*

He searches my face, unclear as to what's shaken me from my post-orgasm haze. "What's wrong?"

"Uhm. Nothing. It..." I stumble over my words. "The time." Shit, how do I explain this? I'm not even sure what the hell I'm doing. "I'm supposed to find my person," I admit with a twinge of frustration. "My soulmate. This year. This December. That's why it's important to me. It's my year."

He stands up, adjusting himself as he watches me move around, pulling my pants back on and trying to right myself from the complete unraveling that just occurred. "Your what?" he asks with a nervous laugh.

Rubbing the back of his neck, I can tell he's trying to figure out what I'm talking about. So, I suppose now is as good a time as any to put it all out there. He was just face first, mouth open, in my pussy. And now, I'm about to douse him in something that sounds complicated.

"There are people who will be here. For the Winter Solstice. People who *might* be my people. Or person." I start moving down the spiral staircase, looking around for my boots. Slipping them on, I talk a little louder so he can hear me. *I'm going to ruin this.*

The bells ringing have to be on at least the tenth time now. It'll stop at twelve. At midnight, to mark the day. The shortest day and the longest night, when time feels slower as the sun stands still.

I blow out a few lit candles and turn off the gas to the fireplace. I can't stay out here. I'll want to stay with him if I do. I'll want more. I won't be able to walk away—shit, I can barely do it now. "I am supposed to remain open-minded. But I've...I've gone ahead and gotten all caught up in—" I search around for my keys to lock up, and my hat.

When I realize he hasn't moved or asked any more questions, I glance around and find him smiling at me.

With his big arms crossed in front of him, he leans against the doorframe, holding my hat in his hand. Repeating me, he says, "Gotten yourself all caught up in what, Aurora?"

Instantly, I smile. He knows what I'm going to say. "You."

"And now you're telling me, you have other people here who are going to be fighting for your attention?" The way he says it makes my stomach flutter, almost like it's a challenge or a lighthearted game. Only, it's not a game.

"In a way." I move to take my hat from his outstretched arm, but he doesn't let go. When I try to take it from him again, he smiles and pulls it back, yanking me against him. I want to listen to what Tash said. To keep an open mind and give today a chance. But how do I ignore this? *This* feels so different. *He* feels different than everyone else. "I don't know what to think. Because I want to go back up there..." I look up to where we just were. "And I want to carry on with what we just started. But–"

He looks around my face and brushes a few curls away. Pushing them behind my ear, his fingers linger on my neck.

I can't help but lean in and close my eyes.

He hums for a second, a deep, brief sound that has me barely able to catch my breath. Let alone make a smart, calculated decision about what I'm doing. "Before you decide what you want, or if you end up meeting this soulmate, tomorrow, tonight, whenever," he says evenly, "promise me that you'll come and find me first. I'm going to need to know when it's the last time I get to kiss these lips."

I hate the idea of a "last kiss" with him. The thought actually makes me nauseous.

Dragging his thumb along the column of my neck, his hand wraps around the back. His fingers pulse slightly, pulling my mouth to his. It's sure and possessive. And I'm drowning in it. His lips brush over mine for only a moment before our tongues meet, and I can't remember a time when it felt like I couldn't kiss deep enough. I just keep wanting more. Goddesses, he devours me, leaving me punch-drunk and swaying as he steps away and leaves with one more light press of his lips against my forehead.

I touch my lips. It's the only part of me that still feels him fully. Someone else can't be possible. Not after that. How could I kiss anyone else after *him?*

CHAPTER 7

GRAY

"Where are they all coming from?" West asks, standing next to me at the top of the stairs. The doorbell has been ringing nonstop since I woke up this morning. I managed to finally fall asleep for a few hours after pulling myself away from Aurora in the lighthouse. I laid in bed for a good hour thinking about all of the reasons why I shouldn't care if she's keeping her options open. I'm not here permanently. And as much as I keep telling myself to stand the fuck down, I keep standing up, staring, and taking exactly what I want–*her*. If one of those coaching positions comes through, I won't be here. Letting that reality settle around me has my teeth grinding and fists balling up tight. Someone like her wasn't a part of the plan when I arrived here. And just now, the idea of not being here has me feeling like I don't know which one I want more.

I take a pull from the double IPA I just cracked open—tastes like piss. I need something stronger than this watching these people pour in. I'm annoyed and feeling a bit needy, if I'm being honest. I've barely been able to exchange more than a few words with her today.

I watch Aurora check in two more guests. She makes every single person who comes in smile along with her. I want one of those smiles. They laugh about something she's said or take a compliment she's doled out. There's nothing complicated about how she makes people around her seem easier. She's a people person, good with everyone she comes across. It's not a mask or a show, it's simply her. I'm complicated, with plenty of masks to wear depending on the show I need to perform. Most people like me, but I can count on less than one hand how many I like. *Maybe a new one has been added recently.*

"You like her," West says as he takes a swig of his beer.

I give him a side-eye glance. There's no use in denying it. "Yeah." I pause, thinking about just how much. "I like her."

He makes a sound in agreement. "She know you like her?" His question comes just as she laughs with a guy dressed in a nice-looking suit. *I have better.*

"She has an idea."

"Might want to make it clearer, then." He nods as the suit wraps his arm around her lower back and leans in to tell her something only for her ears.

I watch as Tash opens the front door. Nobody is there, but just a minute later, another car pulls up and two more women pour out and into the foyer. I've counted at least thirteen guests checking in today.

Tash asked us to join her for the festivities of Winter Solstice. West was a fast yes, and truthfully, mine was just as quick, knowing Aurora would be running a good deal of things happening this evening. She said it was important that her regulars saw more of us, especially this week. I hadn't expected so many people to pass through Wild Tide this time of year.

West claps me on the back. "C'mon. I need another one. And you need to mark your territory." He nods down at the lounge where Aurora just went. "That suit was a little too handsy for my liking, brother."

"For *your* liking," I mutter as I pocket my cufflinks and roll up my sleeves.

By the time we meander downstairs and into the bar and lounge, the parade of cars continues up the slushy driveway. I watch from the front bay window as women of all different ages pull up and grab their bags from the trunks, traipse up the walkway, and into the house. Aurora greets each one of them with arms wide. They all know each other, and not a single person gives a shit about who I am. I could get used to it.

A throat clears next to me. "Here. My special hot toddy recipe," Tash says, passing me a red mug filled to the brim with the slice of an orange round and cinnamon stick floating on top.

We both look out the front window for a beat before I say, "I thought winter was your off-season."

"For tourists, yes. But these are my girls. I know Aurora told you about the Winter Solstice." She nods toward the driveway as another car pulls in. "They're here for the party."

I look past Tash and over her head at Aurora, who's taking the coats of the last two women who just came in with matching bags and hats. When her eyes meet mine, she smiles brightly, and it hits me right in the gut. It's impossible not to return it. By the pink of her cheeks, my guess is she's thinking about where my mouth was not even a full twenty-four hours ago.

Fuck, I want to be back there. I want her. Almost desperately.

It occurs to me, I didn't ask for the details, only that there was a festival of sorts. "Tell me more about this party."

"We celebrate the seasonal change." She looks around the filled room, and I follow her gaze. "We celebrate the year of life we're getting ready to leave behind and we prepare our hearts for the year that's ahead. It's the longest night of the year, which means we make the most of it. We laugh and dance." She holds up her glass, gesturing. "Drink." As she studies me for a second, I can feel her trying to establish my plans here. "We celebrate with a bonfire, signifying the yule log. In some cultures, it's about the sun being reborn, so we watch the sunrise. And we do it all as a family." Once again, my attention lands on Aurora. "She's my daughter, in almost every way that counts. In the same ways that these women are my sisters. Not by blood, but by moments and memories."

I drink my bourbon, tasting the notes of charred oak and vanilla, trying to prolong the moment and commit to memory. It feels good to listen to the laughter and chatter happening around us.

"You've already figured out that Aurora's something special. She makes the people around her feel so much better than they normally would. She feels so much–an empathetic soul who wants to find the right fit for a happy life."

I understand it. More and more since I first saw her. I've watched her all day long talk to people, laughing and carrying on conversations. I keep thinking that maybe if I'm lucky, I'll be able to snag her for a few minutes.

"There's more to you than just running this place, isn't there?"

"You're a smart man, Gray Turner, so let's not play dumb. If you've heard rumors about me, they're likely true. At least pieces of them."

And I've heard plenty. That Natasha Archer is a matchmaker. That she practices magic and makes men fall over themselves. That she's been kind and forgiving toward people who haven't deserved it. That she helps people have babies, clear out bad omens in their homes, hell, I even listened to a woman in line at the pharmacy gossip about the weekend of debauchery that happens during the Summer Solstice. All of it orchestrated by Tash.

She waves and looks behind me, smiling. When she faces me again, it's like the veil she's had on drops in an instant. With a leveling tone, Tash says, "It's her year. You don't need to believe in what I do, but I know this is Aurora's December. And when she falls, she'll fall hard. It's my job to make sure that it's with the right person."

I heard Aurora say it, but it didn't hit the same way then as it did now that Tash has repeated it. I'm suddenly anxious at the thought of her falling for anyone else. It's not even jealousy I'm feeling; it's worse. "How?" I clear my throat to tamp down the nerves rushing in. "How do you know all of that?"

"The same way you know when a curveball or a changeup is coming." She raises her eyebrows at me. "Part instinct, part learned. But you know when to step, when to swing, and when the bat cracks it just right. You feel it. Then you run as fast as you can."

I try to keep calm about what she's telling me, but part of me wants to push back and fight her on it. Demand that the person Aurora should fall with is me. I don't dissect why or how, but I know it somehow.

"And Gray, I know the same way I knew about your parents," she says, and my breath stutters.

My eyes shift to her, and away from tracking Aurora's movement. I lock my eyes with Tash, willing her to say more. I need more information. My parents always told us they met here, in Wild Tide. Hell, it's the reason I've been investing in businesses here. For them. In honor of them.

"You remind me of your dad. He helped build this place."

I rub the back of my neck, trying to shake myself and listen to what she's telling me.

"Did you know that?" Her voice kicks up, as confusion must paint my face. "We had a bad hurricane come through and he had been working for some slacker who was overcharging. So I fired his boss and hired your dad instead. He had an admirable work ethic. He built the top of the oak bar over there." I don't know why I would have never heard this from him before.

"They found each other here. A Winter Solstice match for those two." She gives me a sideways glance. "I wish they'd had more time together. And with you and your brother. I was so sorry to hear of their passing."

I swallow roughly, but the lump stuck there is a big one. It's been years, and I still struggle to rein in my emotions of losing them. With West always around me, it's easy to forget we're such a small family. Just the two of us. It's been that way since I was nineteen and home was wherever we were together. For the past decade, it's been Boston, but now...now, I have no idea where home is or what it should look like. When I take a glance back at Aurora, my chest warms as her eyes lock with mine.

Home is quickly starting to feel an awful lot like her.

It takes another hour for everyone to settle in, and that's just the guests who are staying inside. There are plenty of campers and trailers parked near the lighthouse.

"Goddesses!" a loud voice with a big southern accent croons. "Natasha, is this your new business partner?"

I turn with a smirk as I refill the bourbon decanter. This is the fifth woman who's asked the same question, urging for an introduction to either my brother or me.

Tash says, "Meri, I'd like you to meet Gray Turner."

"Aren't you just yummy!" She claps her hands and wiggles her fingers out at me, pulling me into a hug. "Dahlia, Dahlia," she shouts into my ear. "Come over here and meet Gray."

The woman double fisting two hot toddies approaches with hurried steps. "Gray, such a pleasure. Tash, this is him?"

Tash clips out, "One of them, at least."

Dahlia passes off one of her drinks to me, and then loops an arm with mine. "You get better looking with age." She leans forward to Meri. "See, I called it. When he hit the thirty-somethings, it was all uphill. I told Tash that when you were finally getting some meat on those bones."

I give her a questioning look.

She waves me off. "I knew your mom. Saw some pictures of you and followed your baseball career. Don't worry, I'm not a stalker. Just thought you'd always find your way back here." She looks me up and down. "Interesting that it's now."

It's like dominos. Every greeting leads into the next with women who, in some way or another, had heard of me, but not in any of the ways I was used to. Here, it was because of my parents or Tash. It had nothing to do with baseball or a shitty pop song. Some bring their partners over, and others just come on their own.

"You look nice," Aurora says as she slides next to me, leaning against the bar. When I look at her, my breath catches. It was time to care a little more about how I looked. I wanted her to see me the same way I used to present myself to people who only made me feel a fraction of how she does.

I hadn't seen her in a little while—wrapped up in welcomes and chitchat. The smell of cinnamon and something floral, maybe lavender, settles around her. Wild blonde waves are tied up in braids, with a crown of colorful, dried flowers that I've seen hung around the inn's greenhouse and in the lighthouse. A bright smile tilts her stained red lips, and the only thing that comes to mind is—

"You're beautiful."

Her eyes flare wide, like she didn't expect me to say that. Fuck, I want to tell her again just to see that reaction, to have those lips part for me with another smile.

She shuffles in closer to me.

I lean in, and in a whisper, I say, "Hi."

Trying to keep her smile in check, she sips on her drink.

I can't keep my eyes off her. And people are noticing. I catch glances from a few of the women I met, and Tash, of course. But it's the first time in a long time when I couldn't give a shit. I'm more interested in paying attention to her. The pretty blush taking over her cheeks, and that little dimple dipping in as she smiles.

"Hi," she whispers back.

"Aurora, darling. You look so beautiful," Tash interrupts. She holds Aurora's hands out and studies her and the deep blue, almost black dress that dips low and hangs off her shoulders. Smiling, she says, "This is beautiful," leading Aurora's hand forward to spin her around. "Simply stunning. This one might be one of my favorites."

"You made this?" I ask.

"Altered it. Turned something old into something new." She plays it off like it's no big deal, but I can barely keep track of all the things she creates. It's incredible. The material fits her perfectly, showing off the dip of her waistline and the fullness of her chest. It flares out just past her thighs, and I get stuck on the smooth skin that runs from its edge to her knee-high boots.

Meri and Dahlia come out of nowhere, flanking Tash, both nodding and offering their compliments on the stitching and other things I have no clue about. But it's the tall guy with a sandy brown top knot in business casual attire who has me feeling uneasy and instantly possessive. I don't catch his name, but the Hemsworth knock-off has Aurora's attention when he asks if she's ever been to Montreal. Then he's nodding toward the dance floor. "Will you dance with me?"

She doesn't look to me for approval, and I hate that I wanted it. A claim to her that I know I haven't earned. No matter how much I crave to have her lips on mine again.

"You good?"

I glance at West, realizing I'm squeezing my glass so tight that my hand is starting to sweat. "Depends."

"On?"

"Whether I can convince her that she should be mine."

I know he hasn't so much as flinched since I said it, and he's staring at me. Likely in disbelief. When I shift to look at him, his eyebrows are practically in his hairline and a big goofy smirk is plastered on his face. "You shitting me right now?"

He knows I'm not.

He curls a fist in front of his mouth, holding back a barking laugh and muffling the disbelieving swears that follow.

I move my head slowly from right and left, telling him no. I'm not shitting him at all.

"Look at her," I tell him, just as she laughs. She sways to a slow version of *Let it Snow*. On her worst day, I'd still want to spend my time with her, to see how I can make it better. It's not how I usually feel about people. If someone is having a shit day, give them a wide berth, steer clear, and come back when it's easy. But this pull I feel to her has me thinking all kinds of things I never have, shoving aside the fact that this is supposed to be only temporary.

"I am looking at her." He chuckles. "And it doesn't matter what that guy is saying that's so funny, because she keeps checking to make sure you're still here."

There are a few things I've been sure about in my lifetime. I knew I was meant to play baseball. It was a part of me, threaded into every fiber of my being.

I knew my brother would be my best friend for life the moment I met him. Just like I *know* this isn't something I should ignore with her. I don't even know if I could if I tried.

And I also know that if Aurora moves any further into the center of the room, she's going to be right under the mistletoe, and this guy who's been so eager to be near her will take the opportunity.

I don't fucking think so.

CHAPTER 8

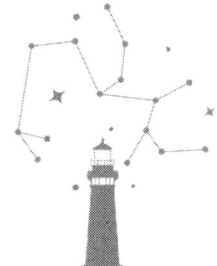

AURORA

"I have a collection of at least two hundred different bourbons," he says matter-of-factly as we tick-tock to the music.

"Really? And do you have a favorite? Mine is—"

"There's a variety of exceptional distilleries that are nowhere near the official Bourbon Trail. I mean, the trail is superb, but you just need to know where else to look."

In an effort to play off his rudeness, I interrupt right back. "I have a really good friend who just started working at a small batch distillery in—" I lose my footing and forget my words as I see Gray coming closer. He looks good. Really good, with even his beard trimmed tight. His haircut makes him look like the cleaned-up ball player I would have initially expected to see. I like both versions of him, but in those navy suit pants that fit perfectly over his thick, muscled thighs, along with his crisp white shirt, tucked in and rolled at the sleeves, he's beautiful. Not handsome or sexy. Hot definitely, but more beautiful than anything. Confidence that always lingers around his aura is out in full force as he heads straight for me.

"I'd love to—" But that's all I hear from the man who was just talking to me. Gray stands right in front of me with his hand extended. And I stop moving. He doesn't ask to cut in or even spare my dance partner a glance. The arrogance makes me swoon a little, and I hate that I'm turned on by the audacity of it. I slide my palm against his, and his fingers clasp tight as he pulls me toward the center of the makeshift dance floor.

People line the room, mostly everyone I've grown up with seeing this time of year. It's not surprising that eyes follow me. They all know this is my year. If Tash hasn't told them, I likely have at some time or another. But none of it matters as Gray pulls me into his orbit. I'm blanketed in the smell of him, similar to the masculine hint of pine and the clean smell of snow. Two of my favorite things.

"Do me a favor?" he says, leaning into me, bringing us closer. His words sound deeper at this volume, and it makes my body buzz.

I only nod yes, because there's not a part of me that wants to move even an inch back from his body. We sway in time with the music, Stevie Nicks' voice keeping time with the sway of our bodies. A repeated rhythm, almost like a lullaby about gut feelings and testing fate. It feels like *our* song, if we had one.

"You got a little too close to that mistletoe."

I lean back to understand what he means. It sounds possessive and like a warning or rule I may have broken. I search his eyes, the prettiest blues and greens, dark and mingling, creating their own color.

The deep gravel of his words is heated when he continues. "Those moments are for me."

"Which moments are those?" I ask softly.

Leaning down next to my ear, he exhales before he says, "Anything that has to do with those pretty lips of yours. Those are mine tonight."

I lean back and tease, "Is that so?" With an innocent smile, I ask, "Which pair of lips are we talking about, Mr. Turner?" I smirk, my fingers playing with the lapel of his jacket. "Both have had the very distinct pleasure of your mouth."

He moves closer to my ear, his nose brushing my jaw.

I suck in a breath as his beard grazes my neck.

"I'm so fucking hungry for both, Aurora. More than you can imagine."

I can't stop the smile that takes over my face, my heart warming just as my thighs clench.

But then, the song changes. It only takes a few seconds as the melody kicks in for Gray's body to stop swaying and go rigid. It's just for a moment, but as soon as it passes, his body language feels off. His hand along my lower back flexes, and his shoulders push back like something has strung him tighter. I pull away from him just a little to see if he's okay.

His neck is red and face flustered. The way his eyes flick around the room for someone. Maybe everyone, like he's waiting for something to happen. And that's when I hear it: *"You're a taker, a breaker, a love faker, but you could never deliver. You could never make her...get there."* The infamous song about the baseball player. And it's so obvious now. I feel silly for not knowing it's this baseball player, *my* baseball player the singer is bitching about. The same man who's searching my face for something that will tell him what I'm thinking. I hate how it instantly turned this perfectly confident man into someone who would rather disappear than dance in front of a crowd for a second longer.

He clears his throat when he sees that I know what's happening. "I can't listen to this song and dance with you."

I don't let him pull away from me, holding him tighter. "This isn't about you. It's about her. And this"—I flatten my palm against his chest—"right here, the way you feel against me, the way you make me feel strong and weak in the knees all at once. This is an *us* moment." Looking into his eyes, the side of his mouth kicks up. It's not a smile, as it doesn't reach his eyes, but it lets me know he hears me. "Stay here with me, Gray. Hold me in your arms and dance to this shit song. And then when it's over, you're going to let me take care of you the way you deserve."

He pulls me closer and buries his face in my hair. I

feel him breathe me in and exhale seconds later, his body relaxing into me. I know what it feels like for people to judge you based on what other people say. Hell, Tash and I have always dealt with it, and I hate it. But I hate it more for him. I hate that he knows what that's like. That it's one of the reasons he's here. To get out of the way of his past with someone and out of the spotlight he had worked for and nurtured.

Tash claps loudly, snapping everyone's attention to the archway that leads into this room. "The Yule spiral is all set and ready, the bonfire is blazing, and I've just poured the mulled wine that Aurora and I made for this year's toast. Please, grab your scarves and hats and come outside."

When I look back at Gray, he's already looking at me. "Go have fun," he says, giving me a chaste kiss.

Nothing like he'd been promising. And that just won't do. Lifting onto my tippy toes, I grab onto the front of his shirt and pull. "Come with me." I smile.

But he resists, and I can tell he needs a minute, even as he brushes another kiss over my lips.

Meri shouts from about ten feet away, "Aurora, can I borrow a pair of gloves?"

"Go. Have fun," he says sweetly, already moving in the opposite direction of the crowd.

I've never been one to school my emotions. Most of the time, they're plastered all over my face. I can only imagine how I'm frowning, watching him move away from me.

"Go," he says with a forced smile, moving back to me

and cupping my face. "But I'll let you take care of me later. Whatever that looks like. Come find me." With a squeeze of my hand, he walks away. I watch as he favors his right knee with a small limp.

There's so much about him I don't know, but I started today by kissing him, and that's how I plan on ending it too.

CHAPTER 9

AURORA

"She's a fourth generation tasseographer, which means she knows a thing or two about symbols and interpretation, darling. Now swirl the damn tea and focus your intentions." Meri rolls her eyes at me, over the owner of Whip & Drizzle. I try to hide my smile at the way Meri has barely any patience with people outside of her close circle of friends. "I swear, Aurora, it's like people have never heard of tea leaves before. I mean, what else are we going to do with them if not read them?"

Tash invited some of her recent regulars to tonight's festivities. Plenty of people from town join us every year, but there's always some who prefer to judge from afar rather than to try something new. Tash would rather have people here and ask questions instead of turning their nose up to something they know nothing about.

I placate her and smile back. "I have no idea, Meri. Seep them and drink them?"

Dahlia pulls her glasses down her nose. "You need more of that mulled wine. Or take a pull from Tash's vape, Meri. It is Solstice, after all. Calm your tits."

Tash comes over just in time with two steaming mugs. "I heard you all the way from across the bonfire," she says to Meri.

She takes it and sips before saying anything else. They only see one another a couple of times a year and yet each and every one of the women who are a part of our circle is like family. Picking up right where we left off.

It takes me a minute to notice Meri staring. When I look and see Tash with the same assessment written all over her face, I know what they're going to say before they even say it. "Go ahead," I tell them.

"Well, I already know it's not going to be the hockey player. Or the one from Saskatchewan," Meri says.

Dahlia chimes in from her seat, "It was Montreal."

Meri bats at the air in front of her, pushing her correction away. "Whatever, he'll be a good fit for someone. That one over there too."

I look over to where she's pointing. "West?"

Tash replies, "Not for you, but that one has an aura that Dahlia couldn't shut up about since she got here."

Dahlia yells as she pokes at the tea leaves in the cup she's reading. "It's true. Brightest colors I've seen in a long time. That's going to be a fun one. I can feel it."

"Aurora, darling, I meant to tell you. Those hand

soaps and lotion bars you have in the bathrooms, they're divine. Can I buy some from you before we leave? Was it orange blossom and mint?"

I nod with a wide smile. "That's right."

Dahlia says, "Oh, I want some too. It smells lovely."

Tash gives me a smile. "Adding your soaps and creams to rooms and in the main bathrooms was smart. I don't know why you haven't done it until now."

"It was Gray's idea—"

"Don't be so quick to give credit away. I like the idea. But I'm proud of *you* for doing it." I stand just a fraction taller hearing her say that.

She looks out around the clusters of friends. Bringing people together is her love language. As much as I've been eager to get to this December, I feel lucky that I get to be here with her. She's been the best family I could have asked for.

"So, you've made your choice?" Tash asks, her expression giving nothing away.

I swallow and listen to the ocean crashing along the rocks just over the ledge to our left. As I breathe in the cold air, I can practically smell the incoming snow. It smells like *him*.

"I don't think I ever really had one," I tell her honestly, studying the flames in the bonfire. "I think even if there was someone already, I still would have been pulled to Gray. I like how I feel when he's near me."

She holds my hand and loops her arm around me. It's cold tonight, but Tash always runs hot. I love leaning in and absorbing some of it. The reality of my life is that Tash has always been the warmth. My home and guardian. "You always have a choice, my darling girl." Sucking in a breath from her vape pen, she exhales a puff of thick smoke. This time it smells like licorice and cloves. The sweet and distinct spice tickles my nose. "Even soulmates." She lets out a deep breath before continuing. "I think the world decided a long time ago that we should only have one. A single person who completes us, but I don't believe that for a second. We become so many people throughout our lifetime. Having just one option seems irresponsible."

I smile at her words as we walk along the path that's been decorated with Christmas greens, from pine and birch to holly and boxwood. It's always been easy for me to understand how complex life can be, that it's not black and white. That the parts of life that are the most honest, most felt, are the ones colored in gray.

"We get a choice. A few soul-level mates, if we're lucky throughout our lifetime, and it's up to us to choose which ones fit best. Sometimes, it's purely in friendship. Other times, it's purely lust and attraction that holds a connection in place. But sometimes, you get both. Sometimes, you get the heat and the heart. The friendship and the chemistry. So, if you think you've found that with Gray, then I don't know what on earth you're doing down here with us old biddies. You should be up there" —she nods at his room—"feasting on that delicious man."

I bark out a laugh. "Tash!"

"What? I told you, you'd find it." She smiles, giving me a wink. "I said this December, by the time the Solstice happened. And look at that"—she pulls out her phone and holds it up—"it's almost midnight. You've already started falling." Pocketing her phone, she kisses my forehead. "It's time to go and land."

I don't linger or waste any more time, because she's right. I've believed in magic for the majority of my life, but I've never felt it the way I do when I'm alone with him. Hell, I feel it even when we're surrounded by a room of people.

I detour to my lighthouse to grab a couple of things first, and then take two steps at a time up to Gray's room. I try to even out my breathing before I knock.

But the door swings before I can catch my breath, revealing a shirtless Gray Turner. He stands there in only a pair of black boxer briefs and the tiniest hint of a smirk. He knows exactly how seeing him half naked instantly affected me. I shamelessly checked him out. If there was time, I would say a silent thank you to whichever goddess wanted to take credit for the impeccable beauty of this man.

He doesn't speak, but the way he looks at me as his eyes track to my mouth has me sweating under these layers. I want nothing more than to shed every single one of them. I search his face to gauge how he might be feeling, if there's any collateral damage after leaving earlier, affected by that damn song. But as soon as I think it, he opens the door wider, signaling me to come in. Biting my lip, I duck under his arm and brush past him into his space. I'm instantly surrounded by the smell of him, masculine and strong, arousing yet calming.

The bedroom suite isn't large, but the couch and bar cart perched across from the bed makes it feel more like a studio space. The fireplace in the corner is lit, but the crackling of the burning wood isn't the only sound vibrating throughout the space. I smile. Christmas music plays softly from the speakers on the coffee table.

He closes the door and locks it as I shed my scarf and coat. I sit on the edge of the bed as he makes his way to the far side of the room to the couch. A perfect view. I can hear every unspoken demand. The way we're both hyper aware of the other is more like a prelude to what is coming. Unzipping my boots, I toe them off, taking my time.

When I look up, I find Gray, manspread on the couch. And I'll be honest, I'm here for it. With his legs wide and arms draped along the back cushions, he watches me. I told him I would take care of him tonight, and I plan to do exactly that. In fact, the promise of it and all the ways it can be interpreted has every single one of my senses working overtime.

My hair is still woven with dried flowers, but I reach up and remove a few pins that let the curls unravel and fall in a curtain behind me. I keep my eyes trained on Gray, the way he returns my interest, feasting on the anticipation of my promise to him. His tongue glides along his bottom lip, and just the reminder of what it feels like to have those lips and tongue exploring me, tasting me, driving me over the edge, makes me shiver.

As it works its way along my spine, I decide exactly how I want this to go.

I pull at the hidden zipper on the back of my dress, and then slip each sleeve a little lower. I hold Gray's eyes for only a second more until I slide the bodice down to my waist. It was an off-the-shoulder dress with cups sewn in, which leaves me in nothing more than a pair of thin silk shorts as I pull the remainder down my thighs.

He hums in approval, a deep tone that hardens my nipples and sends a rush of heat right to my core. Shifting slightly, his legs spread wider. I can see exactly what I'm doing to him. It's addictive to watch your person physically react to every move and wait on bated breath for whatever might be next. Stepping out of the pooled dress at my feet, I make my way to the bar cart. Once I grab a small tin filled with something I made just for him, from my coat pocket, I proceed to pluck a scotch glass and pour.

The air in the room is so thick with tension and wanting, I can barely breathe. And I don't want to if it means I'd burst this intensely sexy moment we're having. The vulnerability from downstairs is long gone as his hungry gaze follows me.

I stop right in front of him, taking a sip of the bourbon and letting it coat my tongue and throat. His eyes drag down my body slowly, so slow that I can feel it along my skin, from my neck to my breasts and down to my belly. The feeling of his attention, the excitement it pushes through my body, swirls lower as his eyes stop right at the hem of my dark blue silk shorts.

I hold out the glass in front of me. "Want?"

He looks at the glass, and then back to me. The man is brimming with confidence and charisma. It drips off him, and I want a taste. Like it heard my thoughts, his cock moves, and my eyes flash to his lap. A smirk lifts his lips, but he keeps his arms draped along the back of the couch and legs spread, otherwise unmoving.

"Want," he says, smirking as his eyes lock onto mine.

Taking the glass from my hand, he tips it back, draining it completely. When he leans forward to hand it back to me, he places it on the ground instead, wrapping each hand around my thighs. He pulls me closer so that my shins brush the edges of the couch, the warmth of his touch already making me melt against him. Leaning forward, he rests his forehead on my stomach, his hands wandering higher as his fingers run across the crease where my thighs meet my ass.

"You feel so good." He breathes in deep. "To touch. To be near. I don't understand it, but I like how I feel."

I drag my fingers through his hair. His dark brown strands are peppered with just a few grays. Too few to notice until you're close enough.

He kisses my skin, just above the waistband of my shorts, and then moves his hands up higher, holding me tighter. It feels intimate, less about just cutting the sexual tension that's wound so tight and more about caring for what's been building between us.

When he tilts his head back to look up at me, so much emotion riddles his face that I couldn't even try to decipher it all. "Does that sound crazy?"

So I tell him what I would want to hear if the roles were reversed. "If crazy is a good thing, then no." I smile. "I like the way you listen. The way you look at me and touch me." I reach toward the table where I left my container filled with herbs and oils. The movement has him leaning back onto the couch again, making enough room for me. "I'm exactly where I want to be."

I turn my body away from him and sit, nestling my butt between his legs on the small vacant piece of couch where his legs are spread. He doesn't ask what I'm doing or what I want, but I know he's curious. I flip off the lid of the combination I've made. It's a soothing pain reliever that I've sold for years, but with a few tweaks specifically for him. The smell that permeates the air has all the fragrant properties: rosemary, eucalyptus, and a bit of my favorite variety of cinnamon. Its base is a CBD oil infused with vitamin C and some organic ingredients that have been known to help alleviate the painful edges of an injury like his. It's hardened into the tin, but with a bit of the warmth from my fingers and palms, it melts on contact.

With his injured knee extended, I work a small amount of the balm along the top of his knee, across the thick scar that's still an angry purple.

"This okay?" I ask softly.

His fingers skate down my back, right along my spine. He moves them up and down slowly, like he's working to calm me, when that's exactly what I'm trying to do for him.

"More than okay," he says. I look over my shoulder

and see his eyes closed, smiling. "You can touch me any fucking way you want, Aurora." His fingers move higher and into my hair. He twists it and holds it, pulling back a small fraction, just enough to let his dominant nature sneak in. "But then it's my turn."

CHAPTER 10

GRAY

I held back as long as I could. I knew she'd come to me. No matter who else tried, there was a part of me that knew she'd end up here. I still didn't know if I deserved it. Finding her at my door already had me eager to hold her, fuck her, not let this thing between us lose its grip. Watching her strip almost completely naked, all on her own, was one of the most disciplined series of minutes of my entire life.

I'm drowning whenever I'm in her proximity–no control, just complete and utter consumption. The smell of her, that sweet twinge of cinnamon and that damn frosting that I tasted the first night we met. Too many emotions washed over me with every step she took closer to breaking our tension. Anger about how I reacted earlier came and went as she stood between my legs, bared to me. But as I held her warm body, pressing kisses on her soft skin, it was the release of exhaustion that did me in. Letting go of the pressure to always be smart and plan for the least amount of fallout. None of that matters with her in my arms.

And now, she's massaging my knee with something she's made for it, and I haven't felt this cared for, maybe ever. Everything about her feels so fucking good.

"You've been favoring it more today."

I hum in agreement. "I walked around the property with the architect and was on it for longer than usual. Nothing I'm not used to. Maybe it was the dancing."

Her skilled hands move firmly around the back of my knee and down toward my calf. Every time she moves just a little, her ass grazes against me and my cock fucking pulses for more. "Well, I liked dancing with you. So, I'll make a deal."

I smile and let out a small laugh at the way she says it so sweetly. "Alright. Let's make a deal."

"Every time you dance with me, I'll massage this for you. I'll make sure you're okay." I like that she's talking about something beyond now, beyond tonight. The idea of this being her promise to me, that we dance, and she eases the pain; it's the only contract I'd sign on the spot, without negotiation.

She works her palms up and over my thigh, and I run my fingers down her back with nothing in their path. She's doing all this topless, like her tits aren't a big deal. They are. They're a big fucking deal.

After a few more minutes, her hands slow. Most of what she's worked into my skin is as rubbed in as it's going to get. I sit up and push her curls to the side over her shoulder, and when my lips meet her neck, goosebumps raise over her skin. She lets out an audible exhale, like she's been waiting for my touch.

I move my arms around her and hold her tight again before I extend my hand in front of her, palm side up. "My turn."

She laughs and asks, "You want me to read your palm?"

"If you can. If you're not too distracted."

And before she can ask what I mean, I lift her ass slightly from the couch so I can get her to drape her legs over each one of mine. She faces out, her back to my chest, holding one of my hands in hers while I shift my legs, spreading hers wide open.

My cock presses into her backside as I move my free hand up her belly, then her breast, and around her nipple. It puckers as soon as I get close. I love seeing her body respond to my touch.

I drag my lips along her shoulder and up the back of her neck, reveling in the contented moan that parts her lips like a sigh. "Tell me what you see while I tell you what I feel."

She leans on me, rubbing her ass against me as she holds my hand flat. Breathlessly, she says, "Your life line has a big deep arc, which makes sense. You're strong, active. And athletic." She releases another moan as my other hand cups her breast and rolls her nipple between my knuckles. "Gray," she whispers. Every breath she takes and exhales has me growing harder.

Making her feel good, taking care of her the way she's so intent on taking care of me, is the only thing I'm interested in.

"I could do this all night. Touch you like this. Hear you trying to catch your breath every time I play with your nipples. Look at how pink and pretty they are." I nip at her ear. "Keep telling me what you see, and I'll give you more."

A shiver runs through her. "Your heart line is long—you're likely to be a good lover. Dominating, but sweet and romantic."

I ghost my fingertips along the edges of her skin, the curve of her breast, circling her nipple again, teasingly slow. "You know what I feel when I touch you?" I mumble into her neck, then drag my lips higher to just below her ear.

She hums in response.

"It's more than just the softness of your creamy white skin. It's the way you move just enough so my hands and fingers can have more. Your body craves my touch, just like I feel this need to hold every inch of you."

Her head tilts back, resting in the crook of my neck. She whispers out, "More..."

I circle my fingers around the nipple of her right breast again. "And tease, and pinch..." I pluck at the pretty raised nipple I had just been caressing. She jolts in my arms, but sinks back with a barely audible whimper. "Keep reading, baby girl."

She lifts her head from my shoulder, just enough to bring attention back to the hand she's been holding. I kiss along that same path of her neck, her skin tasting sweet.

"This line arches up toward—" She sucks in a breath as I nip at her skin. "Gray, I'm so turned on, I can't..."

"What does that arch mean?" I ask, ignoring her. She wiggles in my lap but continues.

"Not many people have this arch. It means you feel things in a big way. That you're sensual, so much so that you can feel restless. But–" She lets out a breathy moan as I graze my fingers down between her breasts and over her belly, dancing them right above her pussy. She rolls her body, eager for more of my touch. A whoosh of air escapes her opened mouth as I push aside the hemline of her shorts and lightly move my fingers around the wet lips of her pussy. I've wound her so tight she can barely catch her own breath. She moans again, this time leaning back into me.

She's such a good girl, she carries on with reading the palm she's still holding. "When someone hurts you, it's not easy for you to get over it and move on. You take your time with things. You want love, but have a hard time receiving it. Accepting it."

She turns her head so she can look at me, those beautiful hazel eyes wide and glassy, as if all the emotions she has are brimming to the surface without permission. She searches my eyes for just a moment before I drag my fingers across her clit. Her eyes close at the teasing circles.

I can guarantee she'll never be able to read another palm and not think of this moment—my fingers exploring her body, teasingly previewing just how explosive we are together.

Knowing she's exactly what I want. The way I'm touching her and the sounds she's making is something I never knew I craved, but now that I've got it, got her, I'm addicted.

"You're the best present I've ever opened, baby." Her body is wound so tight, all it'll take is my fingers to have her unraveling. I slap her pussy—once, twice, three times, and she's whimpering. She's so wet that when I thrust my middle and ring finger into her cunt, I glide in with no resistance, circling right over her G-spot. I bite at her shoulder as she moans, legs shaking. It only takes a minute before her body jerks against me, my name gritted out between her teeth before a small scream floods the room.

"Gray," she whispers out. With a smile in her tone, she repeats my name. "Gray…"

I smile against her skin as she tries to roll her hips for more friction. "The sweetest girl I've ever met is such a needy little thing. Look at you trying to take more." She moans in response and moves the hand she's been reading right against her dripping pussy. "Tell me what you want."

Widening my legs, I open her up even more for me and rub my thumb in punishingly slow circles. She arches her back, and it bows off of my chest as she whines for more. "To fill me. Every way you can." With a shaky exhale, she rolls her hips forward.

I pull her tighter against me and dip one finger in.

"Fuck, you're so wet." I can't think about anything other than feeling her unravel around my fingers.

"More," she whines. Reaching down and back, she fumbles for my cock. "I want you to fill me, Gray. Right now."

"You ready for me, baby?" I push out a breath and hold her body to mine, lifting her hips just enough so I can pull my cock out from being trapped between us.

"Yes," she moans, and my length twitches against her ass. I'm throbbing. "So ready."

I lean back into the couch so the angles are just right. Her back to my front, on top of me, and legs spread wide on either side of mine. "That's it, rub that pussy all over me. Coat my cock in your frosting, baby girl." And dammit, she listens.

I bite at her shoulder, needing to taste and mark in the most primal way.

"I want you so badly, I'm on the verge of screaming." Her chest bows out, and on an exhale, she begs, "Please, please, please." It's the throaty whisper and pleading words that have me losing any sense of control. I'm not capable of holding back from her any longer.

"Tell me this is okay. Taking you just like this," I grind out, rubbing against her.

"I want this. I want you inside of me, please. Ple–" But she doesn't finish, because it turns to a moan as I slide into her all the way to the hilt.

And the noise I make, a groan from the depths of my chest, takes my breath away. She's so fucking tight and warm and drenched, I'm going to embarrass myself.

"You feel too good to drag this out." I close my eyes tight, trying to focus.

If she hadn't already been like a damn fantasy, she says, "Good. Then fuck me. Fuck me so hard that I'll still feel you long after we've finished."

Jesus. At that, I drive my cock deep, and it robs her of coherent words. Me too, if I'm being honest. She's not just getting a hard fuck; she's going to get exactly what she's demanded.

There's a part of me that wants to turn her around and see her unravel, to watch her come apart as I fuck her, but there's time for that later. So I rub the slowest circles on her clit with my free fingers, the other holding her up to move the way I need, while she plays with her tits. I can barely see it happening as I look over her shoulder, but I love that she's not shy about making herself feel good too.

"You're perfect. That's it, baby, play with those pretty tits."

She rolls her hips forward at my words and drops her head back on my shoulder. "Gray." When she breathes my name, it urges me to fuck her harder. Make her feel every inch of me the way that she begged. I spread my legs wider, opening her up and hitting her deeper.

I'm going to make her fall completely apart.

"You're everywhere. So deep. So... soooo good."

I'm fucking thrilled that I can show off exactly how my regimented leg days, even after retirement, have paid off. Her curves are thick and biteable, and I'm about to fuck her exactly how she deserves. "Your body is so beautiful, Aurora. Look at how well you're taking me."

She moans at the praise, lifting and grinding her hips in rhythm with mine.

I hold her ass up higher, just enough to give me enough space to move.

Dragging my cock out of her, I feel how she grips me, even spread open like this. I hold her tight, just inches above my hips, and fuck her furiously, driving up into her from tip to hilt. And I can feel it, the pulsing around my length, her body tensing and trembling, her breaths stalling. She's not just going to come. She's going to tip over an edge that I don't think she's fallen from before.

A moan tears from her throat, quickly turning to a plea. "Fuck, oh my goddesses..."

But I don't let up. She's going to drench us in her release. Our bodies slick with sweat, my grunts quieting, and leg muscles straining, I can feel my orgasm cresting right alongside hers.

"Gray!" she yelps as her body jerks above me. Her orgasm coats us both just as I spill into her with a roar. Seated deep and barely able to catch my breath, I fall so hard that I don't know if I'll ever come back from that. She said she wanted to feel me long after, but I don't think I'll ever feel anyone else ever again. Not after tonight.

CHAPTER 11

GRAY

"You're a little furnace," I mumble into a face full of curls. There's snow falling outside, big fat flakes that stick to the windows and then melt seconds later, thanks to the fireplace in here. And likely this ball of heat snuggled up next to me.

She laughs. "I run hot. Always have. Maybe that's why I love this time of year so much." Smiling, she looks up at the ceiling. The diamond in her nose catches the light, and I can't stop from staring at her as she ghosts her fingertips along my neck and up to my jaw, playing with my beard.

With half of my face buried in the pillow, I'm teetering on the edge of dozing and falling asleep. "Hmm, I like that," I say in a daze. She's managed to make me come three times in a handful of hours. The refractory time in itself is mind-blowing. I shouldn't be surprised; one look at her, and I'm half hard, regardless of where I am.

"What do you usually do for Christmas?"

I raise up onto my elbow to answer. "It's always a little different. It's usually West and me planning something last minute on Christmas Eve. Sometimes a friend will join us at one of our favorite restaurants, or we'll host a cocktail party in the city. But Christmas day, it's just us. Some years it's been at my place and other years I'll meet him wherever he might have decided to fly off to for a little break. We always watch some combination of *Christmas Vacation* and *It's a Wonderful Life*. Sometimes we'll switch it up and throw in some of those classic Claymation movies too." She smiles and listens as we trace each other's fingers.

"That sounds a lot like mine. It's always Tash and me, but some years we have guests. And Tash always makes sure to invite people who might not have a place to go or call home for those couple of days. And we cook. A lot, but I have so much fun doing it. I always like it when there's more people to cook and bake for." Pausing for a moment, her eyes meet mine. "Will this be where you spend Christmas?"

Before I can answer, there's a banging on the door. From the other side, West shouts, "Gray, you need to pick up your damn phone. Hunt keeps calling me, and it's too fucking early to hear his cranky ass."

I sit up, looking around. Aurora reaches over and hands my phone to me from the side table. With a quick kiss, she steps toward the bathroom. Fully naked. Somehow, my cock sensed it, and even before I could stare at her peachy ass walking away, he's up and at 'em again.

"Let me take you out today," I tell her before she reaches the threshold. "A real date."

"Only if I can pick what we do."

"Deal."

When I catch a glimpse of my phone, there's eight text messages and two voicemails from my agent. I don't need to open them to know it's the news I've been waiting for. He got me something good. And much sooner than I thought after our last conversation. But as I scroll through, my stomach sinks.

> HUNT
>
> New York baby!
>
> Hello, are you there, diva? I said New York! They want you.
>
> The fuck are you, Gray?
>
> I just left you a voicemail. Call me back. I want to run through this contract with you. You're going to want to see the numbers I've negotiated.
>
> Do you not have service in that place?
>
> I just left you another voicemail.
>
> I booked your flight. Call me back NOW.

I run my fingers from my hairline to the back of my neck. The panic of what I've been doing is setting in—forgetting about my reasons for leaving and finding a new reason to stay. It happened so fast, so effortlessly, I didn't even fully realize. When I exhale, the weight that had been lifting over the past week settles heavily back on my shoulders all over again.

I've been alluding to plans that meant I'd be here. I've listened to promises from a woman I just claimed as mine. And now, I'm going to leave? I'm going to keep my plan, simply because she was never supposed to be a part of it...

I bite back the disappointment in myself, feeling sick to my stomach.

I'm not this kind of man. I don't want to be.

CHAPTER 12

AURORA

I have only a few more hours to finish these last batches of orders and get them to the corner market, so they'll arrive in time for Christmas. I don't regret spending the last twelve or so hours wrapped up in bed sheets and Gray Turner. Not for one second. I don't think I've stopped smiling since I left his room. But this looming pile of work is really making me nervous. I should have made more time for this. Taken it more seriously. Maybe if I did, this could really be something of my own.

I'm lost in that thought when I hear, "You look like you've gotten a good romp." Tash leans with her arms crossed in the doorway to the greenhouse.

I smile at the pieces of pine I'm tying up as garnish for the bottles of bath oils. That was more than a romp.

That was the dirtiest, most intimate night of my entire life. Dramatic? Yes. But it's the truth.

And I've felt so sure. So ready, but I still need her to tell me I'm not crazy. That I'm brave for listening to my gut. "Do you think it's too fast?"

Tash sprays a mist onto her orchids. The air in the greenhouse is cooler than usual. "I think someone got busy in here last night. Left the door cracked open."

I yelp out a laugh.

"I'm serious. There was an ass-shaped dirt print on my potting table."

She doesn't rush to answer my question, instead she takes her time, like she usually does, and just when I'm ready to abandon waiting, she speaks up. "Do *you* think it's too fast?"

"It feels more like finally than fast. But conventionally..."

She smiles at me in that comforting way she always does. "Some people don't get it right. I think you can find someone who fits you for a short while, and then one day, they don't. But that doesn't keep me from believing in matching people together. Helping couples." She pauses and looks up at the ceiling. "There was a throuple, in the late nineties. Soulmates too. That was a year or so before you showed up. Not conventional from many people's perspective, but it didn't make them any less meant for each other."

I smile and tie the last piece of twine. I could listen to her stories endlessly. The people she's met and connections she's witnessed. I don't try to dissect any of it. I just appreciate that I get to witness it with her.

"Is he staying then?" she asks, and my heart stutters.

I whip my head up to see what she means. "What? I'm not–" I start to say, faltering slightly as I see the look on her face. Like she knows something I don't. It's only been a handful of hours. How could I have missed something as massive as him not staying? "I don't understand the question. Why wouldn't he? He's an investor here. He would have to be..."

Her eyebrows pinch, like what I'm saying is hurting. The emotion written all over her face almost looks like sympathy. But that can't be right.

The room feels like it's gotten a little colder, so I finish tying the last piece of twine and tape up the final box. And suddenly I realize I have no idea what's going on. I've gone ahead and chosen someone, fallen into bed with him, *goddesses*. I excuse myself from the greenhouse and walk straight outside. I need some air.

Campers and vans that came in for Solstice are still lined along the property. I walk down the path from the house to the lighthouse and look out onto the water.

"I thought he'd be a fisherman..." I mumble to myself.

I don't expect an answer, but I get one anyway. "Thought you were done with fishermen?" Gray says lightly. "Been looking for you."

When I look over my shoulder at him, he smiles, but there's something in his eyes that tells me what I don't want to hear.

"You're leaving."

He stops short, and the puff of visible air that escapes his mouth is all the confirmation I need.

He's leaving.

"I have to go to New York." Pushing his hands into his pockets, he searches my face for a reaction, but it's my gut that's sinking. The high I was riding this morning is plummeting with every second that ticks by.

"Okay," I say quietly. More quietly than I intended.

"I don't know what exactly will come after that, but I have to go. It's the opportunity that I've been waiting for. Patiently waiting for–"

I let out a sarcastic laugh. I know a lot about patience and waiting.

He steps closer and tilts my chin up to meet his eyes. His touch has me relaxing into him despite myself. "You're mad."

"You're perceptive," I grit out, trying my hardest to hold back tears from coming.

When he lets go and steps back, I can't believe this is happening. How could it feel so right, and then last night...? I close my eyes, already trying not to miss him. I whisper, "If I knew..."

He bristles. "If you knew, you what?"

I start to walk away. I'm not good with these emotions. The ones where I have to be angry with someone I care about. I'm usually only upset with people I couldn't care less for, but with him, I can't figure out the right way to react.

He calls from behind me, "It doesn't have to be like

this, Aurora. This is still new. It doesn't have to be bad. We can just let it..."

I stop in my tracks and turn on my heel. "You're okay with this being casual? With sleeping with me and having these moments with me—that are rather exceptional, I might add—and then just leaving?" When he doesn't respond right away, my chest pangs with a dreadful thought. "Oh goddesses, am I like a girl you have when you're here?"

"What?" His face crinkles up, before he barks back, "No."

I ignore it because I'm on a bit of a roll. "I choose you. You! And that means something to me. I just never thought to ask if you had too."

"I feel this too," he shouts after me when I start walking again. I hear him grumble, "dammit," and then he's jogging up next to me. "But I'm not *supposed* to be here."

I let out a hopeless laugh just as my eyes water beyond control. "Says who?" I keep moving through the house and into the greenhouse. Grabbing my boxes, I head out toward the truck. I still need to ship these out. When I make it through the foyer, I see Gray sitting on the stairs, elbows on his knees and hands raking through his hair.

"I've been waiting for this, Aurora," he says, with his bags packed next to him.

How did this happen in just a matter of hours? This can't be right.

He looks up at me finally, eyes glossy and brows

furrowed. "I've played ball my whole life. I can't accept that it's done now." For someone who has been waiting for this special opportunity, and now has it in his grasp, he doesn't look that excited. But what else am I supposed to say?

"I understand."

"You don't." He grips his hair and drags his hands through it. "I've only ever been happy playing ball. Everything else has been shit. Relationships. Friends. Everything," he says gruffly.

I recoil at those words.

"I felt like *me* when I played. And then I couldn't." Sighing, he hits his knee with his fist. "I went from being one of the best players in the league to a fucking joke."

Tears fall down my cheeks as I watch him confess all of this. I hate that he feels this way, that something he loved so much was taken from him. And how much *less* like himself he feels because of it.

"I don't know who I am if I'm not playing baseball, Aurora."

I let that sit for a second, taking a breath. To try to comprehend how that must feel. To be so good and revered at something that it becomes part of you. And then one day, it's not and you have to start all over.

"You're the man I met in the kitchen at midnight. I didn't know you played baseball when I met you. I didn't have any clue who you were outside of that moment when I felt you watching me." I bat away a tear and stand up taller. "You can be more than one thing, Gray. I don't know when you decided that your life meant you had to choose which type of happiness you get. You can be more than a ballplayer. I thought a partner, *my* partner, could be another one of those things."

He looks at me with so much emotion that I'm on the verge of wrapping my arms around him to comfort him, but I can't. He's the one making this decision. A decision that I don't want or apparently have any say in.

"Aurora," he whispers out.

The way he says my name guts me.

I'm not going to draw this out. I'm barely holding it together. I've always just allowed things to flow and happen as they will. So much of my life I never question; I just accept it for what it is and move forward. But I can't just accept this.

"What changed?" I stand up taller and bat away the tears that have been crawling down my cheeks. My body is shaking from the adrenaline and the range of emotions that are at war beneath my skin. "We went from wrapped up together in bed, making each other feel good... I've never–" I stop myself and shake my head. I can't even finish the words: *I've never felt this good. I've never felt so connected and right with someone.*

But it's not until I meet his eyes, glassy and pleading with emotions that he's trying to hold back, that I realize he won't give me an answer. At least not an answer or reply that'll make any of this right or different. He's leaving and there's nothing I'm going to say that will change it.

I clear my throat, trying to stamp his face to memory,

because who knows when or if I'll see him again. So I'll say goodbye instead.

"I've loved every single moment with you, Gray Turner. I could have taken millions of moments more, and it probably wouldn't have been enough."

He slams his eyes closed for a moment before opening them again to meet mine. Exhaling a shaky breath, he leans forward, elbows on his knees as he whispers out, "Me too, Trouble."

And it's those words, that silly nickname, that pulls a sob from my throat. He looks down, breaking our connection, and I feel it. Like it was the last bit of him ripping away from me.

I can't stand here and cry. And I will not be a woman to beg for someone to stay. So, I turn on my heel and hurry out the door as fast as the north winds allow, before I start crying too hard to drive away from this ending.

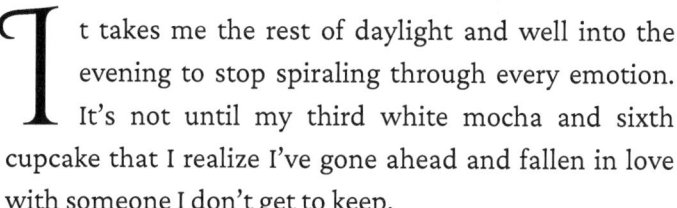

It takes me the rest of daylight and well into the evening to stop spiraling through every emotion. It's not until my third white mocha and sixth cupcake that I realize I've gone ahead and fallen in love with someone I don't get to keep.

Soulmate or not, there's some kind of magic between us that I wouldn't have been able to ignore, even if I did know he was leaving. It wouldn't have changed anything for me. And I should have told him that.

"Which one is it?"

I look up from my spot at the window counter to realize Luna is talking to me.

"Which cupcake?" I look down at the remnants of what's left. "I really liked the one that had the blueberry frosting."

She smiles and stands beside me. Luna's mother inherited Whip & Drizzle from Luna's grandmother, but I know for a fact that it's Luna who does most of the baking now that she's not in school anymore. "I didn't mean the cupcakes, but good to know. I like that one too." She smiles. "But I meant the Turner brothers. The one from the docks?"

I laugh, and she does too.

"They are both the most interesting things this town has seen in a while. Yeah, the one from the docks."

"Gray." She nods. "I see the appeal. Broody and a little rough around the edges."

"Why are you asking?"

"Just curious." She smiles devilishly. "My mom mentioned some of the things she could remember during the Winter Solstice party. Came home covered in dirt when I was brewing coffee this morning."

"Why didn't you come?"

She fiddles with her hands a bit and says, "You know I'm not a party person. I had early morning things to do here." She lifts her shoulder. "But it sounded like a great time."

"Luna," I call after her just as she steps behind the counter. "We're friends, right?"

Nodding, she smiles brightly. "Only one I've got," she says matter-of-factly.

"So you'll tell me if I'm..." I have to look up for a second and reel my emotions in.

She squeezes my forearm, letting me know she's here and listening.

"This is my December," I tell her, eyes watering. No matter if I look up or close them, these tears are going to fall. "But what if that's it? He chooses something else, and I'm stuck with this beautiful memory, but that's it?"

"I think what you've described to me about soulmates and fate sounds like a beautiful story. One that I want to believe in too, but I'm a realist. And I know that some people are lucky to find someone to connect with, even if it's just for moments or only as friendships. I'm sorry he's leaving."

The kindness in her eyes lets me know that whatever she's going to say will serve as a band-aid for a little while.

"As your friend, I'm obligated to tell you that I think Gray Turner is an idiot if he can't see how incredible you are. And if he can't figure out what he's walking away from, then who needs an idiot as their soulmate anyway?"

I push out a laugh. Some tears come with it, but it feels good.

She claps her hands. "Now, I need your help tonight," she says, excitement filling her tone. "I've got a massive order of bread and pastries to prepare, and fate is throwing me a solid by having you here.

Tomorrow is always my busiest day: Christmas Eve eve."

It's the excuse I need to stay away for a little longer. I'm afraid to go back yet, knowing he's gone. For the first time, I feel like believing in fate and soulmates is nothing more than a romantic fantasy. Because if what I felt with him wasn't *it*, that match, the rightness of finding your person, I guess I won't ever know if it's real. Or if I can believe in it at all.

"Tell me what you need me to do."

CHAPTER 13

GRAY

"You've been staring at the dashboard for a while. You okay, man?"

I ignore him, because really, I'm not sure what I am. After I read Hunt's texts, it was easier just to move on autopilot. She said she understood, but I know it's not what she wanted. I squeeze my eyes shut and will back the tears that are really doing a bang-up job of trying to be freed without my permission. *Fuck, what's going on with me? Is this what I want?*

I should be relieved that I've gotten what I asked for —to be on the field again. I should be grateful I get to still be in this sport, do it on my own terms and not be forced into something.

"So what's your plan here, Gray?"

I shift my focus out the window and try to watch the thousands of snow flurries as they move past us on the highway. It's dizzying, much like my thoughts. I try to zone out the uneasy pit in my stomach. The one that's trying to tell me I'm doing the wrong thing. The one I've never tried so hard to ignore before.

You always follow your gut.

"Hunt is supposed to meet me at the office. We'll cover the contracts, and then I'll probably need to start thinking about where I'm going to live."

West keeps flicking his eyes over to me. He knows I'm at war over here. "Just like that?"

Only it isn't *just like that*. When I told her I was leaving, she was surprised because she didn't expect me to walk away. Especially so suddenly too. But I've only just met her. Why would I change everything?

And then I think about how she doesn't hold back. How she put herself out there for me, let me in so easily, welcomed my touch like it was meant only for her.

This opportunity in New York would have only been better had it been with Boston. And yet, even that has a bitter taste. How could I choose bitter when I've already tasted the sweetest, most delicious thing? When she runs her fingers from the nape of my neck and into my hair, I feel it everywhere. The reality of never feeling that from her again has my side pinching in pain.

I shift and look at West, annoyed at the flippant remark. It's been mere days. You don't just fuck with lifelong aspirations over a few days with a woman. *Right?* Right.

"Yeah, just like that," I say back in a sarcastic tone. "Why the fuck would you ask me that?"

"Because I know you. You're going through the motions of what you said you wanted. But you never planned on her. And that's doing something to you. It's fucking with you. I can see it all over your face right now."

I rub my hand against my beard. Fuck, even something as simple as that has me thinking about the way she rubbed her pussy all over it. How she feels pressed up against me and how she makes me feel more like a man somehow. Not a single thing she's ever said to me had me second guessing what she wanted. I tilt back, meeting the headrest. *Fuck*.

"You're not coming, are you?"

He smiles, looking straight ahead at the road. "I like it here. But you know me, I go where you go. If you decide you want to be in New York, I'll be in New York."

It's the first time I feel guilty for wanting him with me. It's the first time I want to tell him he deserves to be where he's happy too.

I can pinpoint the first few mind-numbing beats of the drum and guitar strum, even before the chorus kicks in and vibrates around the truck's speakers. *"You're a taker, a breaker, a love faker, but you could never deliver..."*

"Ah, shit. Sorry, man," West says as he thumbs the button on his steering wheel, rotating to another satellite station.

"It's fine. Honestly..." I let out a clipped laugh. It's not funny, but it doesn't hold the same weight anymore. "You know, we did choose to break up mutually. I wasn't the bad guy she paints here, but she got some of it right. I didn't love her. I took what she was offering and thought that was someone loving me." I run my fingers through my hair again. If I keep doing it, I'm going to end up with a bald spot. "And I've been so fucking pissed off since this shit song came out. But"—I groan to myself because I'm an idiot—"all of it brought me here."

We're less than halfway to the airport, and it's already too far away from a woman who, I can't explain how I know, but I know I'm supposed to be near her.

"Shit, what am I doing, West?"

"Probably figuring out that you should reevaluate your options." The windshield wipers speed up in time with the snow that's falling harder. "I don't think you're getting out of here tonight even if you wanted to. It's really starting to stick."

I pull out my phone and start typing out a text to Hunt.

> GRAY
> I'm not going to make it to New York.

> HUNT
> Don't make me come up to bum-fuck Nowhere, Maine, Gray.

> GRAY
> I don't think it's your speed up here. I'll call you after the holiday.

> HUNT
> What holiday? Why aren't you coming?

> GRAY
>
> Maybe you do need to come up here. It might be good for you.

I smile just thinking about Hunt in this town. Or watching his facial expressions as Tash talks about the power of the moon over a glass of her blackberry brandy. I didn't picture myself ending up in a small town, in a place like Wild Tide. But now I can't picture myself anywhere else.

CHAPTER 14

AURORA

"There's at least a foot out there," I say as I stomp out my boots by the kitchen.

"Still more falling too. Plenty of folks had to hightail it back here. No flights in or out. For tonight, at least. We may end up having a full house for Christmas," Tash says with a double clap.

My most favorite years were always the ones when the inn was full for the holidays. When the days are about relaxing until the next meal. Sharing stories and ideas by the fireplace. Some years, it would be couples who wanted to enjoy a snow-covered Christmas. Other years, it would be folks who chose to not spend it with family. For whatever reason, I liked that we could share the days with new friends. But that's not who I want this year.

I look at her and wordlessly ask the obvious. *Why did he leave?*

"West came back a couple of hours ago, but I haven't seen..."

My eyes water at the realization that he left. The hardest thing to admit, though, is that it doesn't change how I feel about him. There was never a stipulation in finding a soulmate that they would choose you back, just that there was such a thing. A rare and lucky thing to find.

I stared at a lot of flour and eggs for the past few hours, listening to Christmas music with Luna. It helped me arrange my thoughts and make peace with what I still believe in. *Magic.* That it is real, I know it. And while I rarely ask for things at Christmas, I did send out a little request for him to find me again. When the time was right for both of us. Maybe it just wasn't now.

"Can I ask you something, Tash?"

She takes the whistling black kettle off the stove and pours it into two mugs. "Always."

"Has this happened before?"

She watches me for a moment, puzzled by the question.

"Bringing two people together, and it's so..." I sigh because I almost hate saying, "It feels so right, but it's not enough? That it's like you said, time and fate are always at odds. That even with your help, it doesn't end up being that forever kind of love?"

She walks toward me and opens her arms, wrapping me in a big hug. She knows this isn't a hypothetical or a shot-in-the-dark question. I lean in, giving over most of my weight and sinking into her. Rubbing circles along my back, she inhales before pulling back.

"Let me ask you a question," she says, putting her hands on her hips. I nod, already knowing what question she's about to ask.

"What is your gut telling you?"

I tilt my head back and look up at the copper pots and lavender bunches hanging above the kitchen island. "It's telling me that I've met and started falling for a man who is most probably the love of my life, and no matter what might happen, it only feels like the beginning."

She smiles and nods once, like I've just unlocked a secret. "I've known for a long time exactly who would end up setting your soul on fire, my darling girl. Just like I knew it would be this year, in December, right around Winter Solstice. I just needed some support to make sure everything worked out the way that it should."

I know I must look confused, because she smiles before she says, "You know that Meri has always had a little extra influence on the weather." With a shrug, she looks out the window at the big fat snowflakes sweeping by. "And I've always had the lighthouse as my talisman. You feel it, I'm sure, when you're out there, like it has a way of attracting people or, at the very least, guiding people toward us. It always brings the right ones."

I can only stare at her, unsure of what she's trying to say.

"I don't have the ability to change anyone's mind, Aurora, but I am very good at making sure people end up where they're supposed to be." The clock in the great room starts to ding for the time. "And at the right time."

I smile, still not totally clear, until the clock stops ringing on its twelfth chime, and Tash says, "You might want to put those boots back on and ask the man in that lighthouse if what you feel for each other is *enough*."

I can barely see behind the blur of the tears in my eyes as I slip my feet back into my boots, and then swing the side door open. Heart pounding, I fly down the steps and across the pathway, right through the lighthouse door, and into the warm space with lights already on, candles lit, and the fireplace roaring.

"You came back," I say, out of breath, as Gray sits up from the couch. His hair is mussed like he'd fallen asleep while waiting for me.

"I never left," he says, standing, then rushing closer.

I shed my jacket and hat, kick off my snow boots, and instead of waiting for anything else, I keep walking right for him.

"Got halfway to the airport before I realized—"

I don't let him finish. I jump right into his arms. Even if it's just for now, just for the night, for Christmas, for the rest of December, I'll take it. Even if it's not forever, I'll thank every goddess endlessly for letting me know what *this* feels like.

His big hands catch me at the waist as I wrap my legs around him. And he holds me tight, like he can't allow even a centimeter between us.

"Can I tell you something?"

I smile into his neck, nodding yes.

When I pull back, I can't help but touch his beard. I drag my fingers along his jawline and trace down the side of his neck. He closes his eyes, tilting his head into my touch.

"I like that," he hums, and it's like my whole body warms in response. A beat goes by before he says, "I never planned on this, on you." He shakes his head, his voice deep and raspy. "Not the same way you planned on me. But I know a good thing when I feel it." He looks around the room, cluttered with lit garland and books, crafts and wrapping paper. "This life you've built here, it feels like home to me. *You* feel like home to me. My plans and Wild Tide, these are things we can figure out. Together."

That was all I needed. Before he can say anything more, I crash my lips against his. Gray's lips meet mine with the same sense of urgency, like he has to have me the same way I need him.

He moves us backwards, toward the daybed. I'm still wrapped around him as he sits down and settles me on his lap. Curling a piece of hair behind my ear that must have escaped from my knot, he whispers, "So beautiful," as his gaze explores my face. He rubs his thumb along my cheek. "I'm sorry for not treating what this is between us with the kind of respect it deserves." He cups my face, and I move to kiss his palm. "The way you make me feel..." He shakes his head, arms tightening around me.

I lean in and take his lips. A slow brush at first. And I savor the feel of it. But the sweetness of the moment dissolves quickly into something I'll keep craving as time moves on, I know it. My hips roll into his hard, waiting cock, in time with the languid strokes of his tongue against mine. The memory of his mouth and the way he worked my body has me mewling.

"You're the cutest and sexiest damn thing I've ever laid eyes on, Aurora."

I lift my sweater up and over my head, whipping it somewhere across the room, knocking over the small glass bottles I use for oils and serums.

He draws a path with his fingers from my neck, across my collarbone, and over my heart. Brushing his thumbs along the outer curves of my breasts and across each nipple, like he's mapping a path. I want all of him. Every last touch he wants to give, I'll take.

Pushing his fingers up along my back, they caress my neck and then dive into my hair. His fingers flex as he grabs, commanding and strong, before his lips claim mine again. I like the way it feels to be possessed like this. Revered, but wanted. Craved and cradled.

He turns and lays me down on the daybed, blankets rumpled and pillows strewn about. With his eyes locked on mine, he pulls away, rolling my leggings down, taking my panties with them. He doesn't focus on the rest of me, instead our hazel eyes stay connected. Unlooping his belt, he steps out of his pants, his briefs coming next, and then I'm pulling off his shirt.

I smile as he leans up, bracing himself on his arm, leaving just enough space for him to rub his thumb over my clit, causing my breath to catch and back to arch, eyes closing in ecstasy. We've only spent one other night together. It shouldn't feel this familiar, like he knows exactly how to touch me the way I crave. When he does it again and drags his fingers through my lips, sinking two into me, I whimper.

"Let me see you. Open those beautiful eyes."

When I open, he pulls out the fingers he was working inside me. With his eyes locked on mine, I beg for more. "Please, Gray."

"Tell me."

I search his face for what he's asking.

"Tell me," he says with a smirk.

"You feel it too," I say. Words that I asked when I first felt him, kissed him. He didn't answer then. But now...

"I feel it too, Aurora." He captures my lips and seals what he just confirmed, devouring my mouth for all I'm worth.

When he pulls back, both of us breathless and hungry, he taps his cock along my clit. In time with the moan that pulls from my throat, he glides in, filling me. He sinks into me deep, hitting every nerve, and when he's fully seated, he rolls his hips. It hits a spot that feels so exquisite, I open my mouth to tell him how good he feels, how I've never felt so good, but not a single word escapes. The only sounds come from him. A delicious moan as he works in and out of me.

"That's it, baby girl. I feel that too. Your perfect pussy hugs me so damn tight." A groan escapes on his last words.

With Gray's arms caged around me, he's everywhere. Slick skin, warm breath dancing across my lips, the smell of pine and sex flooding all my senses. My orgasm has been waiting along the edges, in my periphery.

"Let me see you come for me." I want to do exactly as he asks. I want to hear him tell me how good I'm doing when I do, and then I want to feel him fill me. He's wound up and ready as he grips me, his hands wrapping around my thighs. Reaching up, I circle my arms around his neck, taking his lips with mine again. "That's it," he groans again. "Your pussy, this body, you're so fucking perfect, baby girl." He tilts his head back, chin up toward the stars. "You're going to make me come so hard."

Kneeling, he pulls me with him, and the angle has his cock so deliciously deep that my body responds with an instant flush of heat and euphoria as my orgasm ripples through me without warning. My thighs shaking, my breath unable to slow down, my pussy pulsing around his cock. It's not until I open my eyes moments later that I see him still watching me as I come down, eyes searing into mine as I whisper out his name on repeat, nails still digging into his broad shoulders. And just as I catch my breath, he falls too, his body flush with mine as he holds me tight, hips rolling and body jerking forward. His moan is low and guttural, and it keeps my body thrumming from the high of it all. My fingers comb through his hair as he finally relaxes as his head on my chest.

"That was—" He exhales heavily and pulls back to see my face. I search his gaze as I trail my fingers around to his forehead, along the bridge of his nose. His eyes close as I move around his handsome features and down through the scruff of his trimmed beard. How easy it feels to care for this man.

"Magic," I whisper to him, finishing his sentence.

He smiles, and with a deep gravel, he lets out a small laugh. Leaning up, he moves his eyes down my body and to where we're still connected. He smirks when he asks, "Want to taste something for me?"

Biting my lip, I nod yes at hearing the request. The same question I asked him the night I met him in the kitchen.

I stick out my tongue and let him drag his finger, coated in our orgasms, across it. I can't help the hum that turns into a moan. His gaze stays focused on my mouth as I feel his cock kick back to life at the sight.

"Tell me."

Smoothing my hand down my body, I draw my finger along where we're still connected. I hold it up, but before I can say anything, he grabs my wrist and pulls my finger deep into his mouth. Closing his eyes, he practically moans as soon as the pad of my finger passes his lips.

"So fucking good," he grits out.

It's dirty and sexy. And I thank all the goddesses because I can't seem to get enough.

CHAPTER 15

GRAY

"Tell them to make their own breakfast," I grunt out as Tash furiously knocks on the lighthouse door.

Aurora stretches her neck, tipping up her chin to look at me. "You do realize you've invested in an inn, where people stay and generally expect some kind of sustenance in the morning?"

"There are plenty of apps that can deliver food," I whisper.

"Not in Wild Tide, Gray. After a snowstorm, on Christmas Eve," Tash says through the door.

I mouth out, "How did she hear me?"

Aurora kisses my neck and moves her hands up and into my hair. Ugh, it feels so good when she does that.

"Aurora, I've already burned a half dozen bagels

somehow." Another succession of knocks come, and she yells out, "Gray, you need to share her today."

My girl smiles lazily into my neck. With her upper half draped over my chest, both of us lie under a pile of warm blankets, practically sweating because the woman emanates heat. What I wouldn't give to lounge in this bed with her all day. We've barely slept. Most of the night was spent making each other feel good.

The other moments when that wasn't happening, before one of us drifted off, we talked about random things. Sometimes important, like the way she'd like to take her apothecary goods more seriously. Sometimes random, like the way the color of my eyes matches one of her favorite crystal bracelets—according to her, it calms and eases anxiety during a period of change. She walked across the room naked and confident, plucking that bracelet from a box and slipping it right onto my wrist. She talked to me about how certain ones invoke emotion while others ward them away. I could listen to her for a lifetime about the things she says hold layers of meaning–rocks, herbs, stars. It's nothing familiar, but I think that's why I like it even more. She's like nobody I've ever met.

"She's right. I need to get up. Tash can barely make cereal, and there's an inn full of people who are going to be hangry pretty soon." My cock is still somehow semi-hard, nudged inside its new favorite place, and I hate the idea of her moving away from me.

"She's busy today, Tash," I yell out.

"Give me fifteen," Aurora yells with a laugh.

She leans up just enough to kiss me, nipping at my lip as she says, "I like you inside of me like this. Keeping you warmed and ready."

I sniff out a laugh. "If you move up like that again, my cock isn't going to let you leave until he's had another run with you. It'll take much longer than fifteen minutes."

The way she laughs, I can feel it vibrate around my body. Her hair is a wild mess, but it's sexy the way it cascades down her back, still smelling like sweet cinnamon.

Just about fourteen minutes later, she's pulling on her boots and that red fringed jacket. "It's Christmas," she says with a smile. Her dimple pops, and it feels like time is an exception when it comes to her. Logically, and in my experience, falling in love should be cautious. But there isn't anything careless about how she makes me feel.

"Did you ask Santa for anything this year?"

"Didn't need to," she says, walking back to the bed and kissing me one more time.

When she looks at me like that, I realize the only person I'm fooling is myself, because I've already fallen for her.

"Can I tell you something?"

She trails her fingers down my shoulder to my chest, resting over my heart. "Later," she whispers. "Tell me later."

I fell asleep for a few hours after that, having not slept that well in a good long while. After a couple of calls, I surface from the lighthouse by the time West is pouring cocktails in the main room of The Timekeeper. He and Aurora had spent the late morning making Christmas Eve appetizers and desserts.

"You look happy," West says as I sample a bite of the stuffed fig that he just finished dressing with honey.

I rub my thumb along my lip, not even trying to contain my smile. "I am."

The kitchen is busy with plenty of guests trying the appetizers as soon as they are served. My brother is a damn good cook. I know he's been eying a few of the downtown properties, so I might as well ask. "Which one do you want?"

He pauses mid-stir, his eyes shooting up to mine. "I liked that spot near the bakery."

"It's yours then."

He chuckles, continuing stirring whatever it is he's mixing up for the next round of appetizers. "I already owned half of those properties. You realize that, right?"

"Well, you can have my half of that one. Merry Christmas."

"Oh my goodness, I was hoping I'd find you boys," Meri says from the doorway. "I see the weather kept you here." She pats my shoulder. "Right where you belong."

Aurora comes up behind me, wrapping her arms around my middle. I lean down, kissing her forehead first, and then those pretty lips of hers.

"Hi," she whispers.

"Hi," I whisper back.

When we look back at Meri and West, their eyebrows are raised and smiles wide.

Meri shifts and pulls out a small book with a worn leather binding. "I wanted to show you boys something. Meant to do it on Solstice, but there was far more blackberry brandy and peyote than I expected." She bats at the air in front of her. "Never mind, not important."

When she opens it, there are pages filled with ribbons and dried flowers, torn pieces of paper with cursive lettering, and pictures that range from black-and-whites to yellow-tinted photos from what look like the 70s. At the top of the page she stops on, it reads: *Winter Solstice 1980*.

"Your mother was already in Wild Tide with your grandparents. They had decided they wanted to spend the winter in Maine," Meri says.

I look up at West, his eyes watery as he looks back at me.

"I brought your father. I had to play a little bit with the weather that year. Dropped a nice little snowfall that caused his truck to veer off of I-95."

"Meri!" Aurora says.

"Don't Meri me. He was fine."

Tash chimes in, "The truck, not so much."

Meri points at Tash. "I had to bring someone for the Winter Solstice, and the one I had planned to bring turned out to be a bit of an asshole. So"—she shrugs her shoulders—"I let fate pick for me. And sure enough, your father needed a ride."

Aurora holds me tighter, looking up at me, smiling.

"This was their Solstice," Meri continues, looking down at the pictures. She takes one out from the fasteners that hold the corners and passes it to me to look at.

"They were a perfect match," Tash says, sliding next to Meri.

"That they were," Dahlia says on her other side.

When I look at the picture, through blurry eyes, there they are. Smiling and happy, which is how I remember them. They look so young here.

"Gray," Aurora says in a soft tone. "Look at where they're standing."

Under a ball of mistletoe in the harbor. A spot where she and I stood just a couple of days ago. I clear my throat, trying to push down the emotion that's crept to the surface. I have plenty of pictures of them, of us together, but there's something special about seeing them here.

West looks at me, wordlessly conveying exactly how I feel. Relieved about being here and seeing this. Missing them. Content in sharing a memory.

"Thank you. It's…" I clear my throat again. "Just, thank you."

Tash reaches across the counter to rest one hand over my brother's and the other over mine. "Merry Christmas, boys. Welcome home."

Dahlia claps her hands. "I think this calls for some hot toddies. Who needs a refill?" She spins around and starts up the teakettle on the stove.

Aurora runs her fingers along my beard. "I'm going to

go help." She kisses my cheek and turns toward the chatter and laughs coming from the main room.

"I knew this place felt right," West says, clapping his hand on my back. He turns back to finishing off the appetizer he was plating. "I'm not going to tell you I love you, but you know...I do. I'm glad you're here."

I give him a smirk. I feel the same, but I can still give him shit for being so damn in touch with his emotions.

"Shut the fuck up, Gray. It's Christmas. I get a free pass to be sentimental."

I smile at the way he's getting so defensive, holding my hands up in surrender. "I didn't say anything." I clear my throat, because as much as it's fun to joke around with him, he's my best friend. "Love you, brother."

He holds up the whisk at me. "That's right, you fucking do."

We talk a bit more about that picture and what it would have been like to have them here. Between the food and company, the rest of the night ticks on in somewhat of a blur. It's the kind of Christmas Eve I'd been missing. The kind I've wanted without realizing.

I run my thumb along the worn leather of the club chair, trying to let the reality of the situation sink in. Only now, Aurora steps around me and sits in my lap. Her red corduroy pants match the red ribbon bow in her hair that's barely doing its job of holding up all her curls. Leaning in, she drags her fingers into my hair. "You okay?"

She smiles, waiting for a response. She's patient with people. She lets silence settle when someone wants it.

She has no idea how the people around her are so enamored with her. And even if she did, I doubt it would change how she treats anyone. She's calm and gentle. But she's the furthest thing from boring. Aurora is wildly passionate and calmingly steady. And...I am undoubtedly in love with her.

"Do you always trust your first feeling?"

She answers with barely a pause. "Yes. I always trust it. Because even if I'm wrong in how I respond to whatever it is, I trust that initial gut reaction to something," she says while leaning closer and holding on to me tighter.

"I haven't. Not in a long time." I grip her chin and pull her lips to mine. When she's this close, it feels impossible not to close my eyes and drift into them.

She hums when I peek out my tongue, drawing hers out. "The first thing I thought when I kissed you in that kitchen was: this is it. *This* is the last person I'll ever kiss. Even if I'm forced to try, it won't get any better than this."

"Gray," she breathes out, peering back and searching my eyes for what else I'm saying.

I pull out my phone and scroll to the email I had been expecting. "These are Opening Day tickets. At Fenway."

Smiling, she listens, her eyes watery and barely holding on to the tears pooling there.

"They'll retire my number. Put on a bit of a show. And then you and I will watch from the seats right behind home plate." I wipe the tears that fall with my thumb. "What do you say?"

She exhales a laugh and nods, knowing how much this means to me. "I'd like that very much."

"Good." I tug her closer and kiss her lips. When I pull back, I finish with my plan and then hold my breath with what she'll say. "I'd like to do that every year, if we can. It's a part of me that I'd like to remember and share with you."

She kisses me again. "Every year, huh?"

"We have time. But yeah, I'd like you there with me. Every year, if we can make it work with Tash and this place. If we have kids, we can bring them too, but—"

She cuts me off, and climbs higher in my lap, wrapping her arms around my neck, and kneeling above me. She kisses me with such an urgency, the rest of the room falls away. The hoots, whistles, and hollers of "get a room!" finally have her pulling back at the same time the ding of the clock chimes. We don't have to look to see the hour. I think both of us already know what time is ours.

With her forehead resting on mine, she says, "I was wrong."

I pull back enough just to see her eyes, searching for what she means.

"It's not just my December. It's ours."

"It's ours," I repeat. Smiling, I fix one of her curls, pushing it behind her ear. *So beautiful.* The way she looks at me, like I'm something special, without the titles that ever afforded me those thoughts and looks before. "I like making plans—having them, keeping them. And I plan on loving you. For as long as time will allow." I wipe the tear that falls down her cheek. "And I'll tell you whenever you're ready to hear it."

The corner of her mouth ticks up, dimple out, reaching all the way to her hazel eyes. "I've been a believer almost my entire life. Love, magic, things you can't explain or see. The stuff you can *feel*." She brushes her fingers along my jaw, through my beard and across my lips. "I feel it with you, Gray. Time doesn't matter. But I'll take those promises you're giving. I'm ready."

On the last chime of that clock, to the twelfth ding that sounded, I said I love you. For the first time, to the last person I'd ever expected, at a time in my life that felt more like an ending than a beginning. But that's what it was, our beginning.

EPILOGUE

TASH

"Is there any chance you can make me some of those delicious little sandwich cookies for our little New Year's Eve gathering this year?"

Luna gives me the smallest hint of a smile. I know she's busy as all get out at Whip & Drizzle, but I have been trying everything in my arsenal to get that girl where I need her to be, and nothing seems to be working.

"I think I can make it work."

"Good. I'll need you to deliver them, and I'll need to have a sampling prior so we can decide which flavors," I tell her as I sip on my first hot toddy of the season.

She shifts her eyes to Aurora. Those two have become as thick as thieves, but Luna's not going to get out of this one. I need her out here.

"Tash, it might make more sense to go to the bakery for a sampling."

I give Aurora a glare. "Wasn't asking for your input here, my darling girl. I'm busy with Solstice tonight, and then Christmas, just a few days from now." It takes her a minute to read between the lines. I raise my eyebrows at her to drive my point home. "And with the new editions on the property, I'm booked on time." What I leave out is that I've had a helluva time getting Luna and her match to be in the same place at the same time.

Goddesses, they really don't make it easy sometimes.

I smile watching Gray come up behind Aurora and wrap his arms around her. "Hey, baby," he says, pressing a kiss to her cheek.

She beams back at him. She's always been an empath, an optimist, but since he came into her life, she's happy. The kind that can have good days and bad days, but they all end in love.

Gray was easily the most famous of my matches to set roots in Wild Tide. He was also the hardest shell to crack. But my Aurora did. In rapid time too. I love seeing them together. So many of my couples don't stay. But they did. And if my interpretation of the moon phases is right and in line with the last tea leaf reading she had with Dahlia, then they'll be raising their little family here soon enough.

It's been two years since Gray and West Turner moved to Wild Tide, becoming part owners of The Timekeeper Inn. I've witnessed Gray and Aurora fall in love and get married right in front of our lighthouse. I'll never tire of seeing the way he looks at her when she's busy making something. Or how she cares for him in ways that have made that man open his eyes and start believing he deserves a full life.

Walking her friend out, I watch the clock and, sure enough, that's when it happens. West Turner comes in just as Luna Douglas leaves. I spy exactly five seconds of a quick exchange. Eyes connect. And there it is. A current that's too fast for most to see. But I was right.

Gray clears his throat next to me. "You have that look."

I give him a side-eye and take a bite of the chocolate sitting out on the counter. "And what look is that?"

"The one where you're plotting. Or whatever it is you do, Tash."

West comes up and steals a piece of the same chocolate. "Hmm, this is good. Is it Aurora's?"

Gray shakes his head. "Luna's."

West hums over his bite. "Might need to order some for the restaurant."

West opened his own small restaurant in town. He does quite well for himself, and I approve because it keeps him out of my hair. One Turner man in close proximity is plenty.

I smile at Gray, and he catches on fast. I see Aurora pinch his arm to keep him from being obvious, because that's the piece that nobody knows. The part that all the movies and books never tell you. We know. We always know which person is meant for the other, but we're only allowed to interfere so much. Agreements made with time and fate long before I ever existed. And it works. Most of the time, at least.

West chimes in, "I swear, Aurora, ever since I started using the dried chamomile and black sea salt mix, it makes the meat so tender. I've had at least a dozen people come back just to tell me how they dream about the meals they've been having."

Her eyes flick over to me, widening.

Crap.

"Why are you looking at her like that?"

Aurora rats me out. "That mix wasn't for tenderizing meat, West."

His eyebrows look back and forth between Aurora and me. Then over to Gray.

Gray holds up his hands. "Not involved."

"I need to go and speak to our guests, see if they're going to stay for the holidays again."

"Tash!" Aurora whisper-shouts behind me.

And then I hear West ask her, "Was I not supposed to use that mix?"

I'm far enough away that I don't hear what she tells him, or if she shares the truth. That the particular mix of herbs and oils he's referring to is what I typically share with people when they're in search of a virile partner. If sex has gotten a little stale and needs a refresher.

I'm an Archer, after all. A matchmaker. The most modernized version of what people believe to be cupid. A person who can see the potential, witness the possibility, and then work her ass off to make sure those fickle bitches, time and fate, get along for long enough so it works out just right.

Magic doesn't have to be something tangible, or even

regarded as special, but it does exist. It could be a moment under the mistletoe, cooking and baking with friends, or sharing a hot toddy with a stranger. But in Wild Tide, Maine, every December at The Timekeeper Inn, there's always a little more magic. Especially at midnight.

THE END

Thank you for reading December Midnights.
I hope the holidays, in whatever way you celebrate them,
bring you warmth and magic... and maybe an extra dose
of heat if you've been nice and a nice little spank if you've
been naughty.

Also by Victoria Wilder

The Bourbon Boys are an interconnected romantic suspense series set in the small Kentucky town of Fiasco. Pour some bourbon dive into the best-seller series.

Bourbon & Lies (Book 1)

Bourbon & Secrets (Book 2)

Bourbon & Proof (Book 3)

The Riggs Romance is a small mountain town series packed with tropes from workplace, second chance, single dad, friends-to-lovers, and more.

A Riggs Romance: Book 1

A Riggs Romance: Book 2

A Riggs Romance: Book 3

A Riggs Romance: Book 4

ACKNOWLEDGMENTS

Thank you to my incredible editor, Mackenzie. I will forever be grateful for having you in my corner and on my team. Gray and Aurora's story turned into so much more than I anticipated when I first started it. They are so much more now. Thank you for helping get them there and pushing me to do better.

To my two wonderful beta readers.
    Amy (@coffeeandbookobsessed), I feel so lucky to have your support. Your feedback, insight, and excellent eye have improved so many of my words infinitely. You're stuck with me now. Kate (@katereadsromance), thank you for your friendship, expertise in the wonderful world of holiday novellas, and for working with me on this story.

To my ARC team of incredible women, thank you for all of your hype, creativity and excitement during my releases. You are such a force for my marketing. I appreciate each and every one of you.

My author friends who take the time to be a sounding board, a resource, someone to vent with, and the inspiration to do this thing that we're doing! Thank you, especially to Alexandra Hale and Julia Connors.

Thank you to my family. To my parents and sisters, I feel lucky that we always had busy and full Christmases that were jammed with more laughter than tears. More noise than quiet. More love than I ever realized. I love you.

Thank you seems repetitive sometimes, but it's equally necessary for my husband and absolutely not enough. But I'll say it anyway. Thank you, my love. And to my kids, for enduring Christmas music in the car since September.

Lastly, to my readers, thank you. Whether you're new here or have been on this ride with me since the beginning, I hope you keep coming back for more. I love writing and can't wait to share all of my stories with you.

ABOUT THE AUTHOR

Forever a hopeful romantic, author Victoria Wilder writes contemporary romance with deliciously witty and wild characters. Her stories range from small-town, swoon-worthy men to fiercely powerful families and lead characters whom aren't afraid to ask for what they want.

She's an east coast girl, living in southern Connecticut with her husband, two kids and Yorkie, Linus. She's always chasing the next season and believes in romanticizing whatever you can along the way. You'll always find her either reading, writing, or ready to dish about books.

- instagram.com/authorvictoriawilder
- tiktok.com/authorvictoriawilder
- bookbub.com/authors/victoria-wilder
- facebook.com/victoriawilderauthor

Printed in Dunstable, United Kingdom